He knew how to torment her....

Shaken by the hot glitter of anger in his eyes, she turned her back on him, slim fingers sliding over the carved glass of the sherry decanter. But his hands went to her shoulders, his grip impressive as he swung her around to face him again, his mouth a slashing stroke of derision as he told her, "There are more ways than one of taming a hellcat," and proved it, bending his head to hers, his lips covering her lips.

DIANA HAMILTON is a true romantic and fell in love with her husband at first sight. They still live in the fairy-tale Tudor house where they raised their three children. Now the idyll is shared with eight rescued cats and a puppy. But despite an often chaotic life-style, Diana has always had her nose in a book—either reading or writing one!

Books by Diana Hamilton

HARLEQUIN PRESENTS
1449—AN INCONVENIENT MARRIAGE
1507—THE DEVIL HIS DUE
1548—GAMES FOR SOPHISTICATES
1563—TROUBLESHOOTER
1588—SAVAGE OBSESSION
1612—A HONEYED SEDUCTION

HARLEQUIN ROMANCE
2865—IMPULSIVE ATTRACTION
2959—PAINTED LADY
2979—THE WILD SIDE

Don't miss any of our special offers. Write to us at the following address for information on our newest releases.

Harlequin Reader Service
P.O. Box 1397, Buffalo, NY 14240
Canadian address: P.O. Box 603,
Fort Erie, Ont. L2A 5X3

DIANA HAMILTON

Threat from the Past

Harlequin Books

TORONTO • NEW YORK • LONDON
AMSTERDAM • PARIS • SYDNEY • HAMBURG
STOCKHOLM • ATHENS • TOKYO • MILAN
MADRID • WARSAW • BUDAPEST • AUCKLAND

ISBN 0-373-11641-1

THREAT FROM THE PAST

Copyright © 1993 by Diana Hamilton.

Printed in U.S.A.

CHAPTER ONE

THERE was something wrong. Very wrong. Something she wasn't being told, she was sure of it. Selina changed down and turned the Volvo on to the narrow lane that led towards Lower Otterley Hall, mindful of the brittle crust of ice beneath the tyres, her golden gaze clouded under strong, arching eyebrows.

But what? She flipped down the sun visor, shading out the low, slanting rays of the pale afternoon sun as they shimmered through the bare branches of trees and hedgerows, spangled now with ice as pure as crystal. She sensed undercurrents and she didn't usually imagine things. She was far too level-headed to worry about anything until it actually leapt up and hit her between the eyes.

So why the decidedly uneasy and definitely uncharacteristic sensation of looming disaster? Selina shook her head unconsciously, setting the riotous mane of tawny, gold-streaked hair flying around her face. It wasn't the current recession which was hitting the King's Ransom chain of boutiques as hard as every other high street business in the land, that was for sure. They had ridden the last and they would come out of this one, too.

True, her buying budget had been slashed, but all that had achieved had been to provide her with the sort of challenge she thrived on. She had only just returned from a two-week buying trip to the Continent, picking up fine leather accessories, summer silks and cottons at knock-down prices. Haggling was the name of the game when times were tough, she assured herself, her wide mouth quirking upwards in a wicked grin. And if the suppliers wanted to keep the goodwill of the ultra-successful, entirely family-owned King's Ransom chain then they had to bend a little, cut profits as the family itself was having to do in order to safeguard jobs and keep shops open and cleverly stocked for when boom-time came again, as it surely would.

As always, when the oddly pitched lichen-covered roofs, the tall, intricate chimneys and the mellow stone walls of the Hall came in view Selina's normally prosaic heart performed a lilt of sheer delight. Swinging the sturdy car on to the long, tree-lined drive, she suffered a sudden, stabbing remembrance of the day when she had first come here to live. Ten years old, her features too bold for her pale little face, her unruly hair tamed into a single thick pigtail, she had been bewildered, battered by the grief of losing both her parents in a motorway pile-up, the cruel waste of which could still leave her shaking with anger even now, sixteen years later.

Her mother's much older sister, Aunt Vanessa, Selina's only remaining blood relative, had offered to take care of her, but it had been her aunt's husband, Uncle Martin, who had given her the affection and patient attention her grieving young heart had so desperately needed. Her cousin, Dominic, a year older than herself, had openly resented her presence. An only child, a precious child, he hadn't been prepared to share his parents with anyone. Which was probably why, Selina thought wryly, his doting mother had been especially careful to impress on him that he came first in everything.

Vanessa, astute businesswoman that she was, brilliant hostess and calculating socialite, had a blind spot where Dominic was concerned. The fact no longer troubled

Selina—she knew her own worth—but it did, and always would, quietly amaze her.

And it had been this house itself, Lower Otterley Hall, that had helped her come to terms with her awful loss. Her uncle and aunt had recently moved in at that time, and Selina had never visited the place before. Bought at the time when the chain of boutiques had been expanding, the house had been far less opulent than it was now. But the young Selina had seen beyond the neglect to the enchanting home it could and had become, packed with so much character that it made the mock-Georgian house in Watford which they had recently sold, and where Selina had visited with her parents, look like a cardboard doll's house.

The gradual and careful restoration had fascinated the young Selina and the choosing of suitable period furniture from auctions around the country had been the one thing to bring her and her aunt closer. But it had been Martin King's patience, his gentle, caring support— even more than her increasingly passionate devotion to the beautiful old house—which had helped her come to terms with the loss of her parents and emerge into the well-balanced, confident young woman she was today.

As she garaged the Volvo next to Dominic's snarly red Porsche she sat for long moments softly drumming her gloved fingers against the steering-wheel, wondering if her uneasy premonitions had anything to do with Martin's health.

But surely not. He had a heart condition, diagnosed a couple of years ago, but he was in the care of one of the most prominent cardiologists in the country and, following his advice, was readying himself for retirement, grooming Dominic to take over his position as financial director for the King's Ransom chain.

No—— Her restless fingers reached for her handbag as she let herself out of the car and collected her luggage from the boot. Everything was under control as far as Martin's health was concerned; he was taking things much more easily and, in fact, for the past six months Dominic had taken his place in the company. Even his birthday celebration tonight, which was responsible for Selina's dash from Heathrow instead of doing as she normally would at the conclusion of a buying trip—staying in town overnight and spending the next day at head office—was to be low-key, just the family for a quiet dinner and not the usual glittering thrash Vanessa organised so well.

So there was nothing to worry over, was there? she questioned herself severely as she cut across the cobbled courtyard at the side of the house and headed for the main door, her stride long and purposeful, the hems of her white trench coat brushing her leather-booted ankles.

And any lingering forebodings were quickly dispelled as she entered the huge, softly lighted hall and the familiar welcome of the old house wrapped her in security. The cast-iron woodburner set into the massive stone hearth radiated a comforting warmth, enticing the maximum scent from the bowls of white hyacinths clustered on every available table-top and window-sill.

Dropping her case at her feet, Selina's wide mouth curved into a slow smile as she felt herself relax, truly relax, and Meg, her aunt's housekeeper, walking through from the kitchen regions, called out, 'I thought I heard you arrive. Good trip?'

'Great, thanks.' Selina's smile broadened into the breathtaking grin that, quite apart from her tall, lissomly feminine body, her striking features and untameable riot of tawny hair, had the power to stop the male of the species in their tracks. 'Where is everyone?'

'Out. Except for Dominic and he's shut up in the study with orders not to be disturbed.' Meg's bony shoulders rose in a throw-away shrug. 'Dinner's at eight, as usual. You haven't forgotten it's your uncle's birthday?'

'What do you think?' Selina was used to Meg's need to organise everyone and everything around her and, as she shrugged out of her trench coat and smoothed the lapels of the rich brown fine wool suit she was wearing, she did some organising on her own account. 'Be a love and bring a tray of tea to my room, would you, please? I need to shower and crash out for a couple of hours if I'm to be fit company for anyone this evening. Oh——' She paused, halfway up the wide oak staircase, her suitcase in one hand, her coat hooked over her arm. 'If Dominic surfaces, tell him I want to talk to him, would you?' He would be able to set her mind at rest as to the state of the business and then she could finally rid herself of the last remnants of the niggling unease which had begun to infect her three days ago. And then, her voice studiedly casual, she added, 'Everything been all right here?'

'I'd have told you if it hadn't been,' Meg answered impatiently and then, relenting because it wasn't like Selina to attempt subterfuge, she always led straight from the shoulder, Meg replied to the underlying question more softly, 'Your uncle's fine. Even without you to keep a strict eye on him he hasn't been overdoing things.' Noting the way the faint trace of anxiety lifted from those long-lidded golden eyes, the housekeeper turned to go and make that tea, passing the information over her shoulder, 'He's gone with your aunt to put in an order at the garden centre—for that enclosed rose garden they've been talking about all winter.'

Feeling inexplicably lighter, Selina went quickly up the remaining stairs. Stupid of her to harbour neurotic anxieties. So unlike her. And she wasn't going to pander to them a moment longer. She wouldn't even bother to ask Dominic if everything was running smoothly as far as the business was concerned. If anything had gone badly wrong he would have contacted her. Or Vanessa would.

So she had a shower, taken quickly, Meg's tea followed by an hour relaxing on her bed before wrapping the carved jade chess pieces she'd found in Rome, knowing as soon as she'd set eyes on them that they'd make a perfect birthday gift for Martin.

Her bedroom was peaceful, right at the back of the house, so tucked away that she might have been alone in the building. Drowsily, she registered a faint chilliness, and wondered whether to dress. Lounging around in a light silk wrap wasn't a good idea, despite the central heating. Filigree patterns of ice were already beginning to form on the outside of the windows as the short winter day darkened to a close.

About to slide her feet to the floor, she automatically reached for the phone on her bedside table as it began to ring out, pushing her rumpled hair away from her face with the back of one hand as she said drowsily, 'Selina Roth, can I help you?'

The tiny snatch of silence from the other end had her wrinkling her brows, becoming more alert, but her wide mouth curved softly as a deeply pitched male voice imparted, 'May I speak to Martin King, please?'

Just a few innocuous words, but oh, what a sexy voice! Thick dark velvet laid over gravel. A voice to conjure dreams of the far-from-innocent variety! Aware of the strange *frisson* that feathered her spine, she took herself in hand and answered, a shade too huskily for her liking, 'I'm afraid he's not here at the moment; can I help you?' A very peculiar reluctance to end the conversation, to go in search of Martin, had her adding, 'I could take a message. Who is calling?' Her uncle might not have returned. As far as she knew, he hadn't, she excused her silly behaviour. Tucked away in her room, right at the far end of the wing at the rear of the house, she had no way of knowing, had she? And again the short and inexplicable silence before that devastating voice sent shivers chasing each other down her spine again.

'Adam Tudor. Tell Martin I'll be dropping in around nine this evening, would you? I won't keep him long. Tell him it's important. Got that?'

'Yes, of course. We'll expect you at nine.' Heavens, what had come over her? Her own voice seemed to be vying with his in the sexiness stakes! As the line went dead she stared at the instrument in confusion before giving her head a tiny shake and replacing the receiver.

She really should have made the effort to put him off, she muttered inside her head as she pushed her feet into her slippers. Sorry, she could have said, but Martin can't possibly see you tonight. She could have asked for his number and told him that her uncle would contact him some time. Tonight they would be holding a private, family celebration. Martin might not want a stranger muscling in, even for only a few minutes.

But he wouldn't be a stranger to Martin, would he? Or not entirely. Adam Tudor had added no explanations as to who he was, which meant that he was known to Martin. And she hadn't even thought of fobbing him off and, always honest with herself, she knew why.

Pulling a disgusted face at her own silliness, she hurried along the quiet corridor towards the main block of the house. She had been curious, she admitted to herself. She wanted to see if the man matched his voice! And the joke would be against her when Adam Tudor turned up in the flesh and revealed himself as being short and fat and definitely ugly!

The suite of rooms her aunt and uncle occupied at the head of the main staircase was empty. Selina checked her watch. Gone five-thirty.

They must have got really involved down at the garden centre, which wasn't entirely surprising since Vanessa had been caught up in her plans for the rose garden for months, infecting Martin with her enthusiasm.

Since her uncle had been warned to take things easily, the dressing-room off the master bedroom had been converted into a book-lined sitting-room where he could sit and relax, indulge his passion for reading, listening to taped plainsong or sharing a glass of sherry with his wife, talking over the events of the day.

Tearing a sheet of paper from the pad on the eighteenth-century rosewood desk, she wrote quickly, the words penned in her distinctive hand, 'Adam Tudor is arriving at nine. He says it's important he sees you', the words standing out starkly against the white background.

She left the note where her uncle couldn't fail to see it when he came in here to relax for a while before changing for his celebratory dinner, then made her way back to her own room.

Stifling a yawn, she slid beneath the comforting warmth of the duvet and curled herself into a ball. She wouldn't sleep. Merely relax and recoup her energies after the last frantically busy two weeks, the flight home and the subsequent drive back here to the Sussex-Hampshire border.

Her mind drifting, she heard again that brief conversational exchange with Adam Tudor and her mouth curved in an unconscious smile. It would almost be a pity to meet the man—his physical appearance couldn't possibly match that fantastically attractive voice! Seeing him in the flesh was bound to be a huge let-down. And, come to think of it, his name seemed strangely familiar. As if she had heard it before... Some time... Somewhere...

'Selina. Wake up, Selina.' Meg's voice penetrated dimly into her consciousness and, as a gentle hand shook her shoulder, Selina opened one eye and then the other, fixing first on the housekeeper's gaunt features and then on the bedside clock which told her it was seven already.

'Oh, hell!' she muttered blearily. 'I didn't mean to sleep.' Struggling up against the pillows, she propped herself on her elbows and Meg said, her voice sounding strained,

'You were tired out. Anyone could see that. Even Dominic said not to wake you.'

'Dominic? What's he got to do with anything?' When had her cousin ever shown any concern for her well-being? If she dropped dead from exhaustion he wouldn't blink an eyelid.

Snapping wide awake now, the knowledge that something was horribly wrong hit her like a blow to the chest, and her voice was thick as she demanded, 'What's happened? Tell me, Meg!'

Her worst fears, the fears that had been wriggling namelessly at the back of her mind for days, now suddenly took on the hatefulness of reality as the housekeeper sat heavily on the side of the bed and, passing a hand tiredly over her eyes, said, 'It's your uncle.' Then, glancing sideways to meet the shock-darkened golden eyes, huge now in a face that was suddenly drained of all colour, she added quickly, 'But he'll be all right. Dr Hill said it was a very mild attack, nothing to worry about in itself—but a warning.'

'But how? When?' Selina demanded sharply, out of bed now, pulling fresh underwear from a drawer, jeans in fine needlecord, a lighter shade of cinnamon than the cashmere V-necked sweater, dressing hurriedly in the first things to come to hand. 'Where is he now?'

'Hospital. Private room,' Meg told her, frowning, getting to her feet and taking a firm, no-nonsense grip on Selina's shoulders, forcing her down on to the carved blanket chest at the foot of the elegant half-tester bed.

Halfway into her sweater and caught off-balance, Selina sat heavily, wrestled the garment into place and caught Meg's compassionate eyes.

'Panicking won't help your uncle. Catch your breath while I explain what happened.'

Closing her eyes just briefly, Selina recognised the wisdom in what Meg said. Her heart was beating like a drum, her breathing too rapid, too shallow. Taking a long, deep breath she opened her eyes again and instructed quietly, 'So tell me.'

'They'd just got back from the garden centre, about a quarter to six, when Dr Hill arrived with a birthday gift for your uncle. A bottle of his favourite port, it was.' Meg sat beside Selina, taking one of the slim, long-fingered hands between her bony ones. 'They were joking about the doctor choosing to bring port so that he could share it while they were playing chess next week. So your uncle invited him up to his sitting-room to join him in a glass of sherry, and the four of them went up—Dominic had come out of the study when he heard them all talking—and, apparently, that was when your uncle collapsed.'

'Thank God Bob Hill was there,' Selina said thickly and Meg nodded quickly, assuring her,

'He was able to do what was necessary and he and Dominic between them got him into his car. Your aunt went with them to the hospital and Dominic followed in his own car. He phoned just before I woke you to say your uncle was stable, that it had been a minor attack. But he's going to have to stay in for a few days—for recuperation and tests.'

'Why wasn't I told? Someone should have woken me,' Selina accused. She was emerging from the initial shock now and couldn't believe that she had been left to sleep, oblivious to all that had been going on.

'I did suggest alerting you,' Meg told her. 'But Dominic said not to worry you. You'd had a gruelling trip and were probably asleep and, in any case, there was nothing useful you could do.'

Except be with him, offer her support to Vanessa who must have been out of her mind with anxiety, Selina thought with silent bitterness, knowing that the truth of the matter hinged on the fact of Dominic's unalterable resentment of her presence in their lives at all. But Meg was saying, 'It all happened so quickly and when they'd all gone there didn't seem any point in worrying you before I got hard news from the hospital.'

'I'm going there now,' Selina stated, crossing the room to retrieve her boots from the bottom of the cupboard where she'd stowed them earlier. She had to see Martin and Vanessa for herself, get the reassurance she needed that her uncle's attack had, in truth, been minor, let

Vanessa know that she, Selina, was ready to offer all the emotional support she needed.

The boots pulled on, she dragged her trench coat from its hanger and reached for her shoulder-bag and was halfway to the door when Dominic walked through, the courtesy of a knock seeming not to have occurred to him.

'How is he now?' Selina and Meg both spoke together and Dominic directed his reply to the housekeeper, his slanting eyes refusing to meet Selina's anxious gaze.

'His condition's stable, as I told you when I phoned, and his consultant will be with him now. He's even grumbling about missing his birthday celebrations.' He gave Meg a thin smile. 'Mother's decided to stay overnight—not that it's necessary, but she insists. Would you pack a bag? You'll know the sort of thing she'll need.'

'Of course.' Meg hurried out without a backward glance and Selina stated,

'I'll take it when I drive over. There's no need for you to make the journey again tonight.'

'How awfully considerate,' Dominic drawled, his grey eyes cold. 'After all, the hospital's all of twelve miles away,' he added sarcastically, moving to stand in front of her as she made for the door. 'I think everyone would prefer it if you stayed here.'

'Is that so,' Selina snapped back, her chin up, already searching in her bag for her car keys. It would give Dominic immense satisfaction to allow his parents to think that she hadn't bothered to stir herself to visit her uncle.

He was very immature in a lot of ways. He wanted his parents to himself, he needed to believe that he was the centre of this particular universe and hated the idea that Selina might take anything away from him. He deeply resented the bond his cousin shared with his father and wasn't adult enough to understand that the affection between them took nothing away from himself.

He had his back to the door now, his narrow face vindictive as he barred her exit, his tone spiteful as he parried, 'Yes, that is so! You've already caused too much trouble. One look at you would remind him of what caused the attack in the first place, and heaven only knows what could happen then.'

'Trouble?' She picked out the damning word, the hot colour of annoyance draining from her skin, leaving it ashen, her eyes puzzled. 'What the hell are you saying? What am I supposed to have done?'

Years ago, when they'd been growing up together, Dominic had always tried to pin the blame on his cousin for any childish misdemeanour. It had made his day if he'd been able to put her in the wrong in the eyes of his parents or friends. She had learned not to care, to simply shrug the accusations aside, knowing his lies were rarely, if ever believed.

And now he seemed to be reverting to type, but this was very different. This wasn't an annoying trifle—a broken ornament or window-pane, a few coins missing from his mother's purse. This was serious. She would never willingly cause trouble for the people who had taken her in and given her every care.

'What have I done?' she repeated harshly, and he answered petulantly,

'That note you left him. Within moments of reading it he collapsed.'

'Oh—come on!' Selina almost sagged with relief. She'd been racking her brains to try to discover what on earth she could have done to upset Martin so badly. 'It was an innocuous phone message, I merely passed it on. If you'd picked up the phone first, you'd have done the same. It had to be a coincidence.'

'Like hell it was!' he sneered, glaring at her down the length of his nose. 'If I'd spoken to Tudor first I'd have threatened him with the law before I let him anywhere near my family. And I wouldn't have let Father know he'd had the nerve to phone. You don't tell a sick man that his enemy is about to knock on his front door!'

'Enemy?' She was aware that she was repeating almost everything he said, but could do nothing about it. Dom wasn't making any sense. Martin didn't have an enemy in the world, surely? She'd never heard of Adam Tudor before this evening ... Or had she? She shook her head to clear it, her strong brows clenched perplexedly, and her cousin told her,

'Exactly. The man's a creep. Always on the look-out for hand-outs. He'd do my father down as soon as look at him—ask Mother, if you don't believe me.'

Selina bit down on her lower lip. She did believe him. His words had the unmistakable ring of veracity. And she said miserably, 'I didn't know. If Martin has an enemy I should have been warned. How could I have known if I was never told?'

'Sure.' Dominic levered himself away from the door, obviously thinking better of the accusatory stance he had taken and, in an unprecedented gesture of solidarity, draped an arm around her shoulders. 'I shouldn't have blamed you, but I was upset. Adam Tudor's existence isn't something we talk about. So——' he took the car keys from her unresisting fingers and pushed them back into her bag '—in the circumstances, it would be best if you stayed here, wouldn't it? Give Father the chance to get over the shock of that message before you visit, hmm? Tomorrow should be OK. And when Tudor does show up you can give him a piece of your mind. You can be pretty formidable when roused! But if you're going to have to do that you'll need a few facts—needless to say, you must promise they won't go any further.' He gave her a tired smile, gave her shoulder a final squeeze. 'As I said, the man's an importuning creep, and if he could see Father—all of us—in the bankruptcy courts he'd do it. Not that he'll get that opportunity, of course, I'll see to that.'

'But why?' Selina's golden eyes mirrored her perplexion. How could someone as straightforward and gentle as Martin have made such an enemy?

And Dominic's mouth twisted down in a vicious sneer as he told her, 'Because he's a bastard. My father's bastard, to be precise.'

It was almost nine. Outside the wind was rising, buffeting the house, roaring through the bare branches of the trees. It was going to be a wild night.

And the wildness within Selina's loyal heart rose to meet it, only to be subdued by an icy determination to treat Adam Tudor with the disdainful contempt he deserved.

After Dominic had left with the things Vanessa needed she had phoned the hospital and spoken to her aunt, apologising for not being around when she'd been needed, asking after Martin, promising to visit tomorrow.

'It happened so quickly, there was nothing you could have done,' Vanessa assured her. 'Your uncle knows that, and he'll look forward to seeing you tomorrow.'

'Dominic explained,' Selina said quickly on a fresh wave of a guilt which, even though she knew it to be misplaced, she couldn't entirely get rid of. 'I'm so sorry.

I would never have passed that message on if I'd known the details—who the man really is.'

'Of course not.' Vanessa's voice was tight and Selina guessed how painful the subject must be for her. 'It's not something we bring into everyday conversation. I take it you're staying there to show him the door if he actually has the gall to turn up?'

'Exactly.' Selina's knuckles whitened as she gripped the receiver, and her aunt said heavily,

'Don't blame yourself. You weren't to know. I honestly thought we'd seen the back of the greedy wretch all those years ago. And be careful,' she warned. 'He could turn nasty. Have Meg around to back you up if he does put in an appearance.'

Which was something Selina had no intention of doing. The fewer people dragged into the affair, the better, and she was quite capable of handling the creep on her own. And Vanessa's reaction had borne out everything Dominic had told her. Every word he had said before he'd left had been burned into her brain.

'Mother's told me a lot about him, but I only saw him once. I must have been about seven at the time. He came to the house—we were living in Watford in those days— and even then, as a kid, I knew he was a threat. Big, black-haired, wild-looking. The aggression was the first thing I picked up. He demanded to see Father. Said he wanted to tell him he had a place at university. And I remember Mother saying that Father was out, telling him that now his slut of a mother was dead there would be no more money. He was eighteen, she said, old enough and big enough to earn his own living like everyone else, and if he couldn't afford to take his place at university then that was tough, but hardly his father's concern. She told him to go. And he did.

'It was years later when Mother told me the full story—how Tudor and his promiscuous mother had tried to drain us dry, how Father had paid a thousand times over for a youthful indiscretion. How he'd been led astray by an older, much more experienced woman. And Father, being the man he is, took her word when she said the child she was carrying was his. Though not even he could bring himself to marry a slut like that, but he supported them both very generously to the end of her life, which must have been just before he came to the house that time, griping because the hand-outs had stopped.'

So Selina was ready for him. The way he had used her, an unknowing pawn, to get to Martin, made her angry enough to kill. The blame for her uncle's attack was his, and his alone. And for that he would have to pay.

He was probably short of money and had decided to try to force Martin to make a handsome payment in return for his silence about their true relationship. Well, he'd be in for one hell of a shock! Mention of bringing in the police would be the least of her threats!

Every nerve working on overdrive, she picked up the sound of the front doorbell and, just for a moment, the supple length of her body as she paced the fine Persian carpet went quite rigid. He was here.

She'd warned Meg to expect a visitor, asking her to bring him directly to the sitting-room. And now Selina braced herself, forcing herself to walk calmly over to one of the tapestry-covered, high-backed armchairs which flanked the huge stone hearth.

Seating herself, she turned her face to the crackling fire and then deliberately took a magazine from the low table at her side, opening it on her lap as she heard Meg's unhurried footsteps cross the huge hall.

When Dominic had recalled that importuning visit they hadn't been living here. When the creep saw the quality of this house and its environs he would probably double his demands! Her ears aching with the strain of listening for his approach, she disgusted herself by remembering how she'd warmed to his voice, how her body had quickened at its sensual quality—how she'd lain in bed fantasising about the man, wondering if his looks could possibly measure up to the way he sounded.

Hastily, she thrust the unwelcome memory aside and composed her striking features into a mask of icy hauteur. Whatever he looked like, Adam Tudor would get what was coming to him!

And then he was actually in the room with her and, totally oblivious of Meg's formal, 'Adam Tudor to see you, Miss Selina,' her breath shook in her lungs.

He was everything his voice had promised, and more. No sign of the down-at-heel, surly weakling she had begun to half expect. No sign at all.

He was six feet plus of male perfection, packaged in a custom made dark lovat suit that could only have come from Savile Row, the white shirt obviously Italian craftsmanship at its best, as were the dark leather shoes.

She made herself stand, forcing the tremor out of her long, long legs, made herself meet the darkly fringed, incredibly green eyes, noting the slashing lines, the harshly crafted structure of his devastingly handsome face, the wide mouth that she instinctively knew could be as cruel as it was sensually fascinating.

Swallowing thickly, she ignored his outstretched hand, the greeting murmured in that unbelievably seductive voice, and tilted her chin a fraction higher.

Dominic had been wrong when he'd described this man as a creep. He couldn't creep if his life depended on it.

That much about him was authoritatively stamped in every line of his face, on every inch of his wide-shouldered, narrow-hipped body. He was a man firmly at the centre of his own universe, who expected to get what he wanted and went ahead and took it.

The fight to get him to back out of Martin's life, once and for all, might be harder than she had anticipated. But it was a fight she was determined to win.

Fixing him with the blazing scorn of her glittering golden eyes, Selina tossed back the riot of tawny, gold-streaked hair that she had spent all her life unsuccessfully trying to tame, and told him, 'I don't know what you came for. But, whatever it was, you are going to leave without it. Right now. And for your sake, Mr Tudor, I hope you understand.'

CHAPTER TWO

SILENCE. A silence so thick, so intense, that for a moment Selina thought the world had stopped.

Then the shaded green glitter of Adam Tudor's eyes stroked her from head to toe, swept slowly up again, lingering on every taut detail of her body, making her cringe inside at this blatant sexual appraisal. But she endured it. Stoically endured this insult, refusing to betray by the merest flicker of anger or disgust that she was aware of what he was doing and so tacitly admit to a compliance of sorts.

The gleam of his gaze rested on the wide, soft curves of her mouth now and she fought to control the betraying shudder of her heated body. Horrifyingly, she felt the muscles at the pit of her stomach tighten as if struggling to contain the flare of flame-hot excitement within, felt her warm breasts peak against the soft covering of cashmere, felt as if his long-fingered hands had followed the path of his caressing eyes...

'Incredible.' The single word hung sultrily on the still, apple-wood-scented air, and she moistened her lips, saw the way his own softened into shocking sensuality as his eyes followed the involuntary gesture, and fought to find the strength to defeat the bastard.

He moved further into the graceful room, his very presence an invasion, but she held her ground. He had to be shown that she wouldn't back away and his single utterance had to refer to her earlier statement, and she reinforced tightly, 'Incredible that you've been shown the door? You'd better believe it. You're not welcome. There's nothing for you here.'

'I wouldn't be so sure of that.' The deep, sexy voice, enriched by just a hint of amusement, enfolded her, compounding the unwelcome *frisson* of awareness that invaded her body as his eyes lingered once again on her mouth.

He was thirty-seven years old and, for the past twenty of them had obviously been fully aware of his effect on women, she reminded herself caustically. And, just as obviously, would have no hesitation about playing on the susceptibilities of the female sex when it suited him.

Well, she wasn't an empty-headed bimbo and was taking his loaded comments at face value. And when he told her, 'But I came to see Martin, initially, that is,' she was able to inform him coolly,

'He's not here. I'm afraid you've wasted your time.'

'I wouldn't class meeting such a delectable virago as a waste of time.' He had the audacity to grin at her, moving closer so that she could actually feel his body heat, could judge the space that separated them down to the last quivering centimetre, and she had to grit her teeth and force herself to stand her ground as he cupped her chin in one warm, dry hand, green eyes gleaming down into seething gold as he asked softly, 'Now I wonder why the lady's so uptight?'

He was using his blatant sex appeal to walk right over her and it was just too much! She despised him, doubly so, for that. And she jerked her head away, out of his hateful dominion, setting her glorious hair flying around her head and her eyes impaled him with the bitter strength of her enraged emotions as she spat out, 'I would have thought that you, of all people, would know the answer to that!' But she had promised herself she wouldn't lose her temper and she tacked on, allowing an edge of ice to rim her voice, 'As I've told you, my uncle's not here. Please leave.'

'I can wait.' The infuriating, slight shrug of those wide shoulders beneath that expensive suiting flicked her on the raw, doubly so as he strode calmly over to one of the armchairs and sat down, his long legs stretched out in front of the blaze from the fire. The time had come for a little plain talking. She wouldn't mince her words, but she wouldn't lose her temper, either.

Following him, she planted herself firmly in front of him and said, on a controlled intake of air, 'Martin won't be back tonight. Probably not for days.' And that much was the truth. But no way was she going to tell him why. If he knew where he was he'd be out of here like a shot, making his demands over a hospital bed!

'Where is he?' For the first time she began to see the man he really was. The teasing eyes were now as cold and still as glacial lakes, the formidable features unreadable, a mantle of power cloaking the superb male body with tensile strength. Whatever he wanted, whatever he had come for, it wouldn't be peanuts.

'I have absolutely no idea,' she lied, her mouth lifting in a small, utterly insincere and worthless smile as she sank with unconscious elegance into the chair opposite the one he had taken.

'I don't believe you.' His voice was a quiet, cool statement of fact and her eyes glinted at him across the dividing space. She didn't care what he believed and felt a reckless excitement welling deep inside her because playing games with this devil could be dangerous.

'Suit yourself. But you're going to have a long, long wait.'

'Again, you're lying,' he stated with smooth contempt, his words accompanied by the slightest lift of power-packed shoulders. 'Did you pass my message on? Stress the importance of my seeing him tonight?'

'Yes.' The word was a bitter condemnation of the effect of having done just that, but he continued smoothly, as if not noticing her abrupt change of tone,

'Then I simply refuse to believe that he could calmly absent himself without seeing me.'

'No? How nice to have such self-assurance,' Selina taunted with cool malice, seething inside at the man's monumental arrogance.

Dominic had said that this creature was Martin's enemy, Vanessa had reinforced that information. And she herself was beginning to understand exactly why they should have received the news of his imminent arrival in the way they had, as if an unexploded bomb had been secreted on their premises. Adam Tudor wasn't the down-at-heel, whining opportunist Dominic had led her to expect. She could have dealt with that. The reality was something else.

A layer of ice inched down her spine as she forced herself to meet his level, thoughtful stare head-on, her golden eyes, long-lidded and slumbrous, giving no hint of her razor-sharp mind as she asked, almost idly, 'How much were you expecting Martin to shell out?' From the suavely elegant look of him, the clothes he wore, he was used to nothing but the very best. Whatever he had in mind it wouldn't be small change.

'I see Dominic and Vanessa have been getting at you.' His beautiful mouth curved humourlessly but there were disconcerting lights in those slightly hooded green eyes that made Selina's breath catch in her throat. She turned her head quickly, looking into the fire, her pure, disdainful profile brushed by the warm glow, revealing the entrancing imperfection of a too short, curling upper lip, the full pout of the generous, made-to-be-kissed mouth. And he continued in that rough velvet voice, as if the question he posed was purely academic, 'I take it your cousin and aunt have also been unexpectedly called away from home?'

How unexpectedly he would never know, not if she could help it. And she despised herself for the way his voice, his looks, his sheer male animal magnetism could make something move deep inside her. This man was her uncle's enemy, for heaven's sake! Merely learning of his intention to visit had been enough to give the elderly man a heart attack! So why did her wretched body react as if this was the one man she had spent her life waiting for when her brain informed her that he was poison?

Her throat was too tight with a disgusting amalgam of sexual awareness and self-hatred to facilitate a verbal response to his question, so she merely nodded, unable to prevent the sideways slant of anguished eyes as they sought his own.

'Then I'm left with no option but to deal with you. Not that that will be any hardship, believe me.' The smoky sexuality of his voice made her heart punch beneath her breastbone, and her hand flew up, as if to steady that wayward organ, and she saw his sultry eyes follow the betraying gesture and went hot all over, her flesh burning.

Belatedly, she hauled herself together and clipped out, 'Fine.' He was all too aware of his masculine potency, of its devastating effect, well used to using it very deliberately when it suited him. And if he thought she'd be a push-over simply because of her gender then that gave her the advantage, didn't it? He would expect her to bend beneath the onslaught of his undoubted attractions, to move to his side of the fence, dragged there by the strength of the magnetic forcefield that surrounded him. He wasn't to know that she would fight for Martin's well-being with every last weapon at her command.

And he was at it again, using that spurious, facile charm as he told her softly, 'I've heard a great deal about you. All of it—interesting.'

Which was a blatant lie. Her job within the company wasn't that high-profile; she did it to the best of her considerable ability but, as yet, it hadn't earned her space in the glossies! And when did a man, such a potently masculine one at that, interest himself in the stocking of women's boutiques? And information about her wouldn't have come from his father, from the family. They couldn't bear to mention his name, much less take him into their confidence.

Clutching at the relief that came from catching him in an outright lie, she was able to consolidate her position of antagonist. Ignoring his lying statement for the flannel it was, she enquired coolly, her eyes watching his impressive features for any sign that might reveal the devious workings of his mind, 'So what is it you want?' and immediately regretted the unfortunate choice of words because his eyes made that silent and very intimate appraisal of her body again while his mouth curved in a slow smile that battered her senses, making her wonder how she would feel if those lips were ever to cover her own. And he didn't give her time to recover her equilibrium, to force the disgust for the type of man he was to smother the growing disgust she felt for herself before he was translating his silent appraisal into words.

'Dinner with you tomorrow night.'

'You must be mad!' The words came out on a jerk of heated breath, colour rushing over her face, staying there as he rose smoothly to his feet, looking down on her, his eyes held in seeming fascination on the hectic pulse-beat at the base of her throat.

'Mad, to want to get to know a beautiful woman a great deal better?' He shook his dark head in a parody of amazement, devils glinting out of his eyes. 'Even if she is a hell-cat.' He turned the full force of his mega-watt smile on her. 'But maybe that's a major part of the fascination?'

She ignored all that for the rubbish it was and repeated stonily, 'Just what was so important about your need to see Martin? Tell me that, and I'll tell you you can't have whatever it is you think you need, and then you can go away.' And never come back, she tacked on in her mind, schooling her features to stony blankness.

And he laughed at her, he actually put back his head and roared his amusement and, if she could, she would have killed him for that alone. But what came next was worse, so much worse that she was left bereft of speech as he calmly walked out of the room after delivering, 'I've already told you. I want to see more of you. Much more.' The lilt in his wicked eyes underlined the ambiguity of that remark and his voice was a rich caress as he told her, 'Dine with me tomorrow night, for starters. Be ready at eight. And if you're thinking of making yourself unavailable then I suggest you winkle Dominic out from wherever he's skulking and ask him if he knows of any reason why you should refuse to meet my demands exactly.'

'What was he getting at, Dom?' Selina shuddered as an icy blast of winter wind gusted across the hospital car park. She pulled up the collar of her coat, her troubled eyes holding her cousin's. 'Why should I see him tonight? Why should I do a single damn thing he suggests?'

Dominic shrugged, his eyes evasive, and, although she had repeated the gist of the conversation she'd had with Adam Tudor the previous night, right down to his parting directive, she sensed her cousin was holding something back, something that was giving him private nightmares.

'Are you sure he didn't give a hint about what he wanted, why he had to see Father?'

Dominic looked almost haunted, Selina thought on an inner shudder. But who could blame him? The trauma of Martin's sudden attack, seeing him lying in that lonely hospital bed, surrounded by wires and machines, his face grey and gaunt, had upset her more than she could say. Even the threat that was Adam Tudor had taken second place in her consciousness, so no wonder Dominic looked haunted, seemingly unable to offer any help.

But Adam Tudor would have to be dealt with, somehow, and she would be the one to do it because she owed it to her family, she reminded herself, shivering again beneath the renewed onslaught of the bitter wind. She thrust her cold hands deeper into her coat pockets and shook her head, telling him rawly, 'No, nothing. I did ask but he didn't say.' Her golden eyes darkened, a frown drawing her strong brows together. 'Just that rather threatening invitation to dinner, and the suggestion that I should ask you if you knew of any reason why I shouldn't do exactly as he said. I've no intention of going, of course. The proverbial wild horses wouldn't drag me.'

'I think you should,' Dominic told her quickly, and her long-lidded eyes narrowed astutely.

'Why?'

'To find out what he's really after, of course. What else?' His face looked white and pinched, and no wonder, Selina thought with sudden sympathy. He would be as worried about his father as anyone, and this desolate car park, the raw grey January skies, the unpleasant subject of their conversation was enough to make anyone look as if the miseries of the world were pressing down on his shoulders.

She suggested gently, 'He's after something. I agree with you there. And we have to discover what it is and keep him away from Martin. But it would be better if we presented a united front. You and I could face him together tonight. He said he'd be at the house at eight.'

'That's impossible.' He looked as if she'd asked him to roll down the street in a barrel. Taking his car keys from his pocket, he tossed them from one hand to the other and told her huffily, as if she were a particularly dense child, 'Now we know Father's in no immediate danger I have to get back to head office. Somebody has to run the company. I'll be staying in town until the weekend, unless Father's condition deteriorates, of course,' he qualified impatiently.

And something of her disbelief that he should leave her to deal with his half-brother must have shown on her face because he reminded her coldly, 'You deal with the creep. I think you owe my parents that much, don't you?' and walked quickly away towards the red Porsche.

Selina gritted her teeth and pushed the wind-tumbled mane of her hair away from her face with the back of a leather-gloved hand. She didn't need reminding of how much she owed her aunt and uncle—her uncle especially. And she would tackle Adam Tudor on her own, if she had to, but she just knew having Dominic at her side would have made it easier and wasn't convinced by his sudden need to rush off back to head office.

In the circumstances, everything would have ticked over quite smoothly in his absence. There were plenty of staff perfectly capable of running the day-to-day business of the boutique chain for another twenty-four hours at the very least. It was almost as if he was afraid of facing his half-brother, listening to his demands and ruling them out of court.

And almost as if she was afraid of facing Adam Tudor again on her own, a cool inner voice mocked spitefully. As if she was afraid of that palpably cataclysmic masculine appeal. Afraid of the way she might react to it.

Which was, of course, absolute nonsense, she assured herself roundly, squaring her shoulders and marching over to where her Volvo was parked, the heels of her leather boots clicking decisively on the tarmac surface. She wasn't a silly teenager to be taken in by a handsome face and a superb male body, or the type of voice that could charm the inmates of a harem out in droves!

Quite why she had informed Meg that she would be entertaining a guest this evening Selina was not altogether sure. That she would feel safer, keeping that unwanted dinner appointment here, on her home ground, conjured up the opposite—fear. But she had already assured herself that she wasn't afraid of him, hadn't she? And when the housekeeper's thin face had registered surprise that Selina should be entertaining at all, at a time like this, she had announced coolly, 'It's business. And make the meal simple; there's no need to try to impress.'

And so it was. Unpleasant business, at that, she reminded herself as she gave up the attempt to tame her abundant hair into a sober knot and allowed it to tumble all over her shoulders. And business that was best conducted on her own ground.

Although she had deliberately dressed down, making no concessions to her femininity, the dark navy fine wool dress she had chosen to wear seemed to flatter her greyhound slenderness, subtly emphasising the sensuality of the curves she had intended it to disguise. Strange. A frown caught the soft skin between her brows. She had never before noticed what the understated, very simple style of the dress did to her figure before, or how the deep, almost sombre colour made her hair look like living flame.

But it was too late to change. It was almost eight and pride wouldn't allow her to keep him waiting. If he was left to kick his heels in the drawing-room he would believe, in his conceit, that she was taking her time over making herself look her best for him.

As she reached the head of the stairs she heard the chime of the doorbell and her heart leapt into her mouth. Meg was already crossing the echoing space of the softly lit hall to admit him. Selina had never felt so alone in her life but she was determined not to let it show as she descended the stairs, her head held high, her eyes carefully fixed just above his left shoulder as he crossed the portal, her voice devoid of expression as she instructed, before he could get a word in, 'Take Mr Tudor's coat, Meg, and we'll eat in half an hour.' There were a few flakes of snow on the shoulders of the soft sheepskin. Her eyes followed Meg as she carried the garment to the carved oak hanging cupboard tucked away beside the main door. And she used those small signs of the inclement weather as an excuse as she said, still not looking at him directly, 'We'll keep that dinner appointment here.

The weather's too foul to think of going out,' and cursed herself for needing an excuse at all, for allowing him to deduce that she did.

And her skin crawled with embarrassed humiliation as he drawled smokily, a smile in his voice, 'Relax. The idea's fine by me. When I need my arm twisting before I'll dine alone with a beautiful woman I'll know it's time I was pushing up daisies.'

So he, the prime egotist, believed she'd decided to entertain him here in order to be quite alone with him! His conceit was beyond bearing!

She turned quickly, hiding the way her face ran with colour, and stalked ahead to the drawing-room. But by the time she'd gone through, noted that Meg had banked the fire up, drawn the long burgundy-red velvet curtains against the wild black night outside she had herself well in hand. And her eyes met his with cool mockery as she put him straight, facing him confidently as she told him, 'Don't flatter yourself. What I have to say to you can be better said without an audience. Besides, I couldn't be bothered to make the effort to go anywhere with you. Sherry?'

And she saw his eyes darken and narrow, his mouth tighten as a spurt of anger made his impressive frame go rigid. So her calculated rudeness had flicked him on the raw and, just for a moment, she exulted in her hitherto unsuspected power to hurt him.

But the unworthy emotion didn't last long because something else took its place, something dark and tormented which sprang into shocking life, spreading its tortuous, poisoned talons into every vein, every nerve-ending, making her soul shake as he said through his teeth, every word tight with menace, 'My God, you're asking for it.' Two furious paces brought him to her side and, shaken by the hot glitter of anger in his eyes, she turned her back on him, slim fingers sliding over the cool, carved glass of the sherry decanter. But his hands went to her shoulders, his grip impressive as he swung her round to face him again, his mouth a slashing stroke of derision as he told her, 'There are more ways than one of taming a hell-cat,' and proved it, bending his head to hers, his lips hard and punishing as they covered hers.

Her head jerked back beneath the ferocity of his kiss but her body was imprisoned in the iron cage of his arms and every last inch of her went up in flame beneath the pressuring contact of his ruthless masculine frame. And it was like nothing she had ever experienced before and as his tongue penetrated the soft inner moistness of her mouth her brain switched off on sudden burn-out and her senses took over, adding to the torment of sweet ravishment as she kissed him back, her body all boneless grace, and pliant, melting into his as his mouth gentled, still hungry, but different, intoxicatingly different.

She was having to cling on to him to maintain her balance and her hands had found their way beneath his jacket, and the feel of his body heat through the crisp cotton shirt he was wearing was intensely disturbing——

So disturbing that when he at last lifted his head from hers she was breathing in shallow, rapid gasps, her heart fluttering beneath her breastbone, her eyes hazed with the effects of what he had done to her senses, barely registering the smouldering quality of his thickly lashed, shadowed green gaze as his own eyes drifted from her parted, swollen lips to the crazy pulse-beat where it fluttered at the base of her throat and down, down to the twin, tumescent peaks of her breasts as they thrust their erotic invitation against the soft wool of her dress.

And slowly his fingers followed the lazy drift of his eyes and her senses leapt in tumultuous, untameable excitement as the pads of his long clever fingers scorched fire down the length of her throat, slipping beneath the V of her neckline to draw soft, slow circles around one thrusting nipple, laying waste her powers of reason, ravishing her senses until she no longer knew where she was. Or cared.

And later she would never be able to say with honesty where the black magic of his sexual onslaught would have led her if the door hadn't opened to Meg's, 'I'm carrying dinner through now, Miss Selina.'

Utter disorientation held her where she was and she was thankful for the way he turned to face the door, effectively screening her from the housekeeper's view as her fingers fumbled in an agonised, uncoordinated hurry to straighten her clothing. And when he stepped casually to one side she caught Meg's straight stare and felt the colour of her overheated cheeks turn to a crimson conflagration, and she mumbled something, she had no idea what, and was too busy trying to cut through the heavy swaths of her utterly shameful and unprecedented sexual arousal with a brain that seemed to have been drugged out of orbit to make any sense of Meg's dour, 'Snow's coming down like you wouldn't believe. I thought I should warn you.'

'Thank you.' It was Adam Tudor who effectively took over, normalising a situation which had all the hallmarks of a nightmare, Selina thought distractedly as he added, 'We'll be right on through.' And one of his hands cupped her elbow lightly, the gentle pressure of his fingers easing her forward as she tried to marshal her mental powers and push his unforgivable, disgraceful behaviour right to the back of her mind.

And, almost, she achieved it because as Meg disappeared she dug her heels in, wrenched her arm from his grasp and, not daring to look at him, not caring to be reminded of—of anything she spat out, 'That was totally uncalled for. Don't ever, ever touch me again!'

Jerking her chin up, she stalked out of the room, the height of her spindly heels making her hips sway. Knowing he was following, just a whisper away, did nothing for her blood-pressure and when she paused outside the dining-room door, and turned, her soft body brushed against the hardness of his and her breath jerked in her lungs and solidified painfully when he told her with arrogant ease, 'Don't spit, little cat. You've just had a sample of the methods I'll use to tame that temper. So sheath those claws and purr for me because, believe me, you ain't seen nothing yet!'

CHAPTER THREE

THANKFULLY, Meg appeared at that moment, wheeling a heated trolley along the passage, but Selina gave him one look of seething, burning hatred before leading the way into the dining-room. She had been right to be afraid of being alone with this devil in human guise; the first encounter with the burning brand of his mouth had been enough to make her lose all control. But there would be no second encounter; she would make absolutely sure of that!

Seating herself, her nostrils flared with a tiny surge of anger. She'd told Meg not to go to any trouble but she'd gone ahead and pulled out all the stops. Despite the adequate central heating a huge fire burned companionably in the grate, the overhead spots doused to leave a couple of rich-shaded table lamps to shed soft intimacy over the panelled room, and pure white candles lent extra grace to the fine Irish linen, old silver and exquisite crystal set before them.

If Meg had deliberately set out to impress Martin's wealth and standing on the stranger then she couldn't have done better. It was just a pity that the last person that should be impressed was Adam Grab-What's-On-Offer Tudor!

'The beef Wellington and the greens are on the trolley,' the housekeeper informed her sniffily, handing out the steaming bowls of walnut soup. 'Trifle, cheeseboard and fruit on the sideboard. I'll bring coffee later.' Sighing gustily, she stumped out of the room, leaving a positive miasma of disapproval behind. Selina smothered a sigh of her own.

Meg could have served cottage pie and fresh fruit in the more informal breakfast-room, which had been the kind of fare Selina had had in mind when she'd told her not to go to any trouble. But she'd perversely put in as much effort as she could, making a martyr of herself to stamp home her disapproval of the fact that Selina was entertaining at all as firmly as she could.

But Meg's long-endured vagaries were pushed to the back of Selina's mind because she could feel that intense, wicked green gaze on her—it prickled right through her skin. But she didn't look up from her soup.

After that degrading scene back in the drawing-room she would have demanded he leave, had ached to do so, but she still had to discover why he had wanted to see Martin in the first place. Raising her head at last because no problem went away if you went on ignoring it, she met his eyes across the table and found a tone of cool enquiry.

'Suppose you tell me why you're here.' And wished in a moment of childish panic that she didn't feel so deserted. She couldn't blame Vanessa for wanting to stay with Martin until she was properly satisfied he was on the mend, but Dominic needn't have fled back to London in such a bone-breaking hurry...

'But you know why I'm here.' The smoky voice was velvet-soft, the green eyes glinting with triumph. 'I wanted to get to know you better, and so far I've enjoyed the progress we've made.' He had finished his soup and was pouring Martin's prized and classic burgundy into Waterford glasses, and Selina stopped pushing the croutons around her bowl and laid down her spoon.

'What did you want Martin to do for you?' she asked tightly, ignoring his unforgivable reference to the way he'd kissed her, the way she'd allowed it, actually encouraged it.

'It's not a question of what he can do for me, rather of what I can do for him.' He was still smiling softly, his voice gentle, as if they were discussing something pleasant and normal and not something devious and sinister, something that had given Martin a heart attack. And the insouciant devil was moving around, collecting the soup plates and reaching for the beef and vegetables, the hot plates from the trolley. As if he owned the place, as if he had rights. And Selina, provoked beyond caution, snorted,

'Do you really think I'm crazy enough to believe that?' She would have liked to punch the facts home, call the monster's bluff, let him know that the thought of a visit from him had put an elderly man into hospital. But she couldn't allow herself that luxury. She had to prevent him from finding out where Martin was, prevent him from turning up at the sick man's bedside.

So she contented herself with staring at him from furious yellow eyes, her arms crossed over her chest, and the fury changed to resentment as, taking over, he calmly carved slices of meat, added a generous portion of vegetables and handed her the heaped plate. Which she ignored.

And then, settling down to his own meal, he asked levelly enough, 'So what have you been told about me?' He speared a piece of tender, pastry-enclosed beef with his fork and sipped Martin's best burgundy with evident appreciation. 'From your reception of me, I take it Vanessa's been getting at you, giving her distorted version

of my character. And I don't suppose Dominic had any
hesitation over putting his oar in the water, either.'

A dark eyebrow rose with half-contemptuous
amusement and she scornfully gave him full marks for
trying, for taking the game right into her court, and told
him frankly, 'I was told that you are Martin's son. That
Martin supported you both until your mother died. By
which time you were eighteen and able to fend for
yourself.' She pushed her untouched food away and
picked up her wine glass, hoping the alcohol would calm
her stretched nerves. 'The general opinion is, I believe,
that you would have liked to receive Martin's financial
support indefinitely.'

She hoped she had put that delicately enough. She
had no wish to pussy-foot around, because from what
Dominic had told her, and from her own knowledge of
the effect his intended visit had had on her uncle, he
deserved all he got. But she had already had one ex-
tremely graphic demonstration of his reactions to the
way she had deliberately angered him before and wasn't
angling for a repeat performance.

'I see.' He laid down his cutlery and gave her an unreadable look. 'And did either of them mention my
mother—apart from the fact that she'd died?'

Selina quickly buried her nose in her glass. Dominic
had. But again, to reveal she'd been told that Adam
Tudor's mother—and why, dammit, did that name seem
oddly familiar?—had been promiscuous, had taken advantage of a much younger man's inexperience, had
tried, throughout the rest of her life to bleed him dry,
and how her son, after her death, had tried to do the
same, had come looking for charity, would definitely
bring his own special brand of retribution down on her
head.

So she held her tongue but it appeared he could see directly inside her head because his face closed up, his eyes narrowing to slits as he repeated, 'I see,' forcing the words through his teeth.

'I'm sorry.' Her mouth tense, she got to her feet. The polite form of words was so patently untrue that she felt like a fool for saying them. And she added quickly, 'You must see that in coming here you're wasting your time, upsetting the family.' That was as near as she could get to the truth, without letting him know what he had done to Martin, and her eyes went cold. She had only one thing on her mind now—to get rid of him, once and for all.

But Adam had other ideas. He stayed exactly where he was but his eyes followed her tall, swaying figure as she walked to the door, and the heavenly voice was cutting as he told her, 'Have you stopped to ask yourself why Vanessa and Dominic painted me black? And don't pretend they didn't. Your reception of me alone pointed to that. And did you wonder why the whole damn lot of them seemed to have disappeared off the face of the earth?' Then, as sanguinely as a prowling cat, he was on his feet, his mouth barely moving as he commanded, 'Come back here. I haven't finished with you yet, not by a long way.'

She flicked her eyes to his and then quickly away again as her heart tightened and shifted inside her. There was a dark magic in the way he looked and moved and spoke, something indefinable that reached right out to her. And she didn't want it to be that way so she fixed her eyes on a point somewhere just above his left shoulder as she took two concessionary paces back into the room and said as coldly as she knew how, 'You're magnifying your own importance.' Her small chin lifted as, against every self-preserving instinct, her eyes were drawn to his wicked green gaze. And although she felt the heat of betraying colour cover her creamy skin she refused to look away, to back down in front of this opportunistic devil. 'My aunt and uncle are away from home and Dominic's tied up in London on the firm's business.'

'Oh, I just bet he is!' Adam drawled, his mouth curling cynically. 'I don't give a damn about him or Vanessa. But it's vitally important I see my father.'

Selina stared at him. What kind of fool did he think she was? And she drawled right back at him, 'Vitally important to whom? Or to what? Your bank balance, most likely! The type of clothes you wear, for a start, don't come off the bargain rail in a chain-store basement.'

The way he looked at her sent a stab of apprehension through her stomach but he did no more than shrug very slightly before he told her, 'If that's what you want to believe, go ahead.'

And strangely, despite what she'd been told about him, the hard facts that all added up to his utter detriment, she didn't want to believe it. But charm, allied to his fantastic looks, was part of his stock-in-trade, and she wasn't going to fall for it, was she? Besides, if what he wanted of Martin was above-board, then there would be nothing to stop him telling her what it was.

'Tell me why it's so vitally important that you see him, and if I agree I'll tell you how to contact him.' Her voice had emerged rustily as she'd issued the challenge, and she knew by the frantic flutter of her heartbeats that she actually wanted to hear that what he had to say to her uncle was innocent of the threat both Dominic and Vanessa had implied.

She dragged in a breath, the tip of her tongue nervously moistening her parched lips, and felt the quick hot stab of something nameless as she watched his half-hooded eyes lazily follow that give-away movement.

His soft smile was tinged with regret but the wicked green glints in his eyes cancelled out the spurious remorse as he told her, 'I'm afraid it's between me and Martin,' and the disappointment was keen, sharp as a knife just for one moment before she thrust it out of existence, because all along she had known—hadn't she just?—how rotten he was. Dominic had called him his father's enemy and never again would she even begin to question that.

'Then we've reached an impasse. And I'm afraid I can't help you, Mr Tudor.' No way was she about to tell this devious swine how to contact Martin, where he was. She would defend the beloved elderly man any way she could. He had been warned to avoid stress and anxiety and Adam Tudor meant just that—stress and anxiety in its most undiluted form!

'Why so formal, Selina? We're capable of being on very friendly terms indeed—I think we've proved that much, to our mutual satisfaction, don't you?' He had started to move towards her and the look in his memorable eyes made his intentions quite plain. He was about to do something she wouldn't like. Or rather, she corrected herself with panicky honesty, something she might like too damn much!

'I'll hurry Meg along with the coffee. You might as well have a cup before you leave.' The words came out on a husky rush and she left the room with more haste than dignity. Then, overcoming the impulse to lean back against the smooth wood of the door, to get herself back together and give herself time to work out just how to ask Meg to stay glued to her side after she'd brought in that coffee, instruct her not to leave her until that devil was safely out of the house, she strode rapidly down the corridor to the kitchen.

But maybe enlisting Meg's help wasn't such a good idea, Selina decided as the housekeeper said stiffly, 'Finished that lot already?' meaning the minor banquet she'd martyred herself preparing and of which Selina herself had hardly tasted a mouthful.

'We're ready for coffee; I'll take it through.' She could ask Adam Tudor to leave the premises all by herself, she told herself staunchly. She didn't have to panic when he looked as if kissing her again was the only thing on his mind. For pity's sake, she had deflected many an amorous male in the past without calling in the troops, and to ask for Meg's support would call for explanations she had no intention of making. Far better to say nothing and endure the older woman's huffy mood.

'You do that.' Meg banged a few saucepans around. 'And I'll go and make up a bed in one of the guest rooms for your man friend. Whether he uses it or not is up to you. But I dare say it will look better if I go through the motions.'

'What the hell are you talking about?' Selina put the filter-coffee jug down on a tray with a crash. Meg was what was politely known as a 'character' and had ruled the family with a heavy hand and sharp tongue for many years, everyone putting up with her moods, ignoring them because they knew she would die for any one of them if she had to. But this was carrying the sharp-tongued-old-retainer bit much too far and Selina growled, 'If you're implying what I think you're——'

'If the cap fits.' Meg's long nose was high in the air. 'It's not seemly—entertaining men friends when your poor uncle's fighting for his life and your aunt's worried half to death and Dominic's working all hours to keep things going.'

'And I'm taking the heaven-sent opportunity to indulge in a bit of sneaky bacchanalia!' Selina supplied sarcastically, fuming at the housekeeper's exaggeration, her gross distortion of the facts. 'It's business. I told you.'

And Meg pushed her chin in the air, her mouth turning down as she snorted, 'I'm not that daft. And I've got eyes in my head, haven't I?' Meaning she'd taken in that torrid embrace, and, that being so, Selina could find nothing to say in her own defence because she had reacted shamefully to his kisses and Meg had walked in on them just as she'd been about to go completely over the top!

Trying to forget the slow burn of colour that crept over her skin, she informed Meg crossly, 'There is no question of Mr Tudor staying the night. He will be leaving just as soon as he's had coffee.' She added cream and sugar to the tray, her hands shaking with temper. One day someone would have to remind Meg of who paid her wages!

'Well, if he doesn't sleep here I don't know where he will sleep,' Meg grumbled, beginning to back down, as she always did, if she sensed she'd gone too far. 'I did tell you about the snow. He could have got out then. Not now. Look for yourself.'

Selina stared at the housekeeper in appalled disbelief, her feet seemingly rooted to the kitchen floor, and, giving her a withering look, Meg clicked her tongue impatiently and marched to one of the windows, dragging back the curtains. 'Well?'

No need to say a thing. What could she say when the outside security lights danced back from drifts and heaps of glittering whiteness, mockingly magnifying the swirling, sticky flakes that were still pouring out of the cold night sky?

'I'll put him in the oak room,' Meg said grimly. 'That should cool his ardour.'

If that remark had been meant to shake Selina out of her trance-like stillness, it failed. Something akin to shock kept her where she was, and speechless. The immense disquiet filling her right now had more to do with her insane reaction to him as a man than the very real knowledge of how bitterly angry both Dom and Vanessa would be when they found out that Martin's son and enemy had been offered refuge for the night. Suddenly she began to shiver.

And Meg said, her tone a touch less censorious now, 'I admit I thought it wasn't right for you to be entertaining a man friend at a time like this. But it wasn't my place to say so. You're a free agent. What rubbed me up the wrong way was the way you lied. It's not like you. Tell the truth and shame the devil—that's always been your style. You shouldn't have told me it was business when I only had to walk in that room and see him mauling you and you enjoying it to know it wasn't.'

If Meg was waiting for an apology, an explanation, she'd wait forever, Selina thought irritably, her spine very straight. How could she tell the other woman why Adam Tudor was here when the truth of his identity was the family's best kept secret? And how could she explain the devil's dangerous sexual potency—a potency so overwhelming that she, who had spent years fending off would-be amorous advances because she had neither the time nor the inclination to get serious at this stage of her life and was sensibly wary of casual sexual encounters, had found herself in a vortex of mindless abandon at the very first touch of his lips on hers?

'Well, I'll say no more,' Meg said thinly into the silence. 'I'll fix up the oak room, then make myself scarce. I know my place!'

Which patent untruth would have been laughable in any other circumstances, Selina thought edgily as the kitchen door closed with a decided thud behind the housekeeper. And then her irritation with Meg transmuted into burning anger against that damned man. It was all his fault! Meg, the abrasive cornerstone of family existence, who had been her somewhat prickly friend for a decade, now regarded her as a sneaky liar! And sooner or later she was going to have to inform her aunt that her husband's despised and feared bastard had not only enjoyed the most lavish hospitality Lower Otterley Hall could provide, but had spent the night in the very best guest room!

Her fingers clenching, she dragged the curtains back over the small-paned window, left the coffee where it was and strode back towards the dining-room, her spiky heels beating an angry tattoo.

Doubtless he had seen this coming. She recalled having seen flakes of snow on his coat so he must have known the conditions were worsening. And he, unlike her, would have had all his wits about him when Meg had made that pronouncement about the increased snowfall.

And so he, the sneaky opportunist, had simply sat tight, waiting to be snowed in. Why? What devious plans were skulking in that well-shaped head?

Selina paused, her hand on the smooth wood of the dining-room door, her mouth compressing. Adam Tudor was a tough nut. Not for him the schoolboyish pleasure of spending a night in his father's home when, in any other circumstances, he wouldn't have been allowed to cross the doorstep. And the reasons he'd given for being here at all this evening—getting to know her better—didn't ring true. The way he'd kissed her, the things he'd said meant nothing. He'd been playing games to mask his real intentions. Of that she was completely sure.

But what his intentions were she had no way of knowing and wasn't waiting to find out. Snow or no snow, he was going!

Her eyes sharp with determination, she pushed open the door, was momentarily disconcerted to see him lounging in one of the fireside armchairs, a glass of wine held loosely in one hand, but when he commented lazily, 'This is nice. Come and join me,' she gathered herself together and informed him frostily,

'Sorry to spoil your fun, but you're going to have to dig yourself out,' tacking on with perverse enjoyment, 'I'll point you at a spade while you brace yourself.'

And he had the barefaced audacity to floor her with the sweeping power of his slow, lazily intimate smile, his eyes narrowing to emerald shards of amusement as he drawled, 'No need to get your knickers in a twist, sweetheart. While your sense of hospitality—not to mention your manners—leaves more than something to be desired, your excellent housekeeper comes up to scratch.' He took a long, sybaritic swallow of Martin's wine and added airily, completely ignoring the fury that brought her strongly arched brows down to the bridge of her nose, 'Meg just dropped by to let me know about the white-out. She mentioned something about the oak room. Now, why don't you accept defeat gracefully and join me, as I suggested?'

She'd rather join a hungry shark in a bath-tub, and his use of the word defeat meant that, slowly, the gloves were coming off. Defeat meant games where there were winners and losers, and yes, maybe he'd won this battle, but she'd make good and sure he lost the war!

She had been fighting battles all her life—at least, ever since she'd been orphaned. As a child it had taken courage to accept that she was no longer the centre of anyone's universe because the two people who had loved her best in the world had been taken from her. And later it had taken a different kind of courage to take the lonely career road she had chosen rather than opt for a relationship with one of the many men who'd shown interest simply for the security of being one part of a couple.

So she was used to winning battles. Trouble was, she reflected uneasily, so was he. The laid-back charm that seemed to surround him like an aura did absolutely nothing to mask the steely determination beneath. But she wasn't going to think about that, and as he finished his wine she sent him a cool look, took the glass from his hand and put it firmly down on the table, telling him, 'I won't pretend to be ecstatic about it, but I'll show you to your room.'

She had expected resistance, expected the smooth-tongued charmer to surface, insinuating that the night was still young, that the fire burned brightly and the candles dimly, that there was still plenty of excellent wine in the bottle. But he got to his feet, indolently panther-like, and she took a hasty step backwards, putting distance between them and, to cover that Freudian giveaway, said briskly, 'Perhaps you'd like to use the phone to let someone know what's happening. Your wife?'

'I'm not married, if that's what you're asking.' Green eyes mocked her as the wicked mouth curved in a taunting half-smile, and she turned on her high heels, her voice controlled as she headed for the door.

'I'm not interested enough to do that. I was merely extending a little of the common courtesy you accused me of lacking.'

She set off across the hall at a lick, knowing that any semblance of poise she had was in danger of deserting her. He was keeping effortless pace, his devilish amusement surrounding her like a prickly blanket. She wasn't used to being laughed at and hated the sensation of having events slip out of her control. But, she reminded herself roundly, she was in charge. All she had to do was show him to his room, take certain precautions and wait until morning when the council would have cleared the lanes and the farmer, a few fields away, would, as he always had done in the past in similar circumstances, bring his snow plough to clear the long driveway to the Hall.

The oak room, situated at the head of the main stairs, was, in Meg's words, enough to cool anyone's ardour. She'd been ten years old when she'd come to live here and for a couple of months the only words her cousin had spoken to her had been, 'Shove off, can't you?' But then he'd started following her around, whispering about the ghosts that haunted the oak room, ghoulish stories that had made her hair stand on end, given her nightmares. And when he'd dared her to spend the night there on her own, creeping along the corridors after his parents had retired for the night, she had known she had to take up the challenge. With a perspicacity beyond her years she had known it was the only way to get him off her back, put an end to the torment of those whispered stories.

And she'd done it, too! Even now she felt proud of that much younger self, of the way she'd closed the heavy hangings of the carved four-poster bed and read *The Wind In The Willows* from cover to cover by torchlight. And, after that, she'd had Dom's measure. He had never been able to bully or frighten her again.

She was twenty-six years old now, had carved out a solid career for herself, knew where she was going. If she had been able to handle Dominic when a mere child she could handle Adam Tudor. Just see if she couldn't! And she was almost grinning when she opened the door to the sombre, oak-panelled room, the heavily carved bed with its muffling hangings set in centre-floor state.

'I do hope you'll be comfortable,' she said with sweet sarcasm, turning to make her escape before he could get a word in. If there had been a key in the door she would have locked him in for the night, and he must have read her mind again because his husky voice followed her, taunting her,

'Don't break your neck in your rush to lock up the family silver—it's far too pretty.'

Hateful man! He was far too astute for her peace of mind and the first thing she did was go to the study where Dominic and, sometimes, Martin worked on files brought home from head office. Her full mouth firm, she activated the Hall's security system, put the handful of folders Dominic had left lying around in the safe, sat behind the desk and pulled the phone towards her and punched out the numbers of the apartment the family occupied when they had to stay in town.

But Dominic wasn't answering. Out at some nightspot entertaining the current expensive lady friend, she thought with a sigh of exasperation. He went for both quality and quantity, his tastes running to delectable model girls with mercenary inclinations. Never anything serious, Vanessa usually saw to that, but sometimes Selina despaired of him, she really did. Couldn't he see that the progression of lovelies that trooped through his life were only interested in what they could get out of him?

Giving him the benefit of the doubt, she tried the office and, predictably, got the answering machine. Not bothering to leave a message, she locked the door behind her and went through the dining-room. She'd try the apartment later. He had to be told that Tudor was here, muscling in where he definitely wasn't wanted. Even if he wasn't prepared to actually put in an appearance and throw his half-brother off the premises he could advise her on how best to handle this turn of events. They could talk things through; two heads were often better than one.

The fire was burning low now so she put the guard in front of it, loaded the used dishes on to the trolley and pushed it through to the deserted kitchen. Meg had obviously taken herself and her disgruntled mood off to bed and Selina made a mental note to get up early enough in the morning to warn the housekeeper not to talk about Martin's heart attack in front of Adam Tudor. Not that she was likely to do any such thing, Selina thought as she loaded the dishwasher, pouring what was left of the wine and sipping it as she tidied the kitchen, but it was better to be sure than sorry.

There had been more wine in the bottle than she had realised, she thought woozily as she doused the kitchen lights and made her way up the back staircase to her rooms. But at least the intake of alcohol on a practically empty stomach might help her sleep. Though somehow she doubted it. Doubts and anxieties about what Adam

Tudor was actually up to were running around in her mind like hysterical rabbits, and that wasn't conducive to restful sleep. So a soak in the bath might help to relax her, besides helping to pass time before she could reasonably hope to contact Dominic back at the flat.

The back stairs led directly on to the passage that led to her wing of the house. Even now, she couldn't imagine why, as a lonely and unhappy ten-year-old, she had chosen a room as far away from the other occupants of the Hall as she could possibly get. But, showing an understanding and sensitivity she would always be grateful for, Vanessa and Martin hadn't turned a hair, had gone several steps further and given the whole wing over to her use, creating her own special world, the bathroom, bedroom and playroom furnished with things she was familiar with, brought from her old home.

Now the playroom had been transformed into a high-tech office where she often worked, rather than use head office and the London apartment, and the frills and flounces of her little-girl bedroom had made way for her now more sophisticated tastes.

Nevertheless, this wing was still her own special place, inviolate. She always felt more relaxed here than anywhere else she knew. And gradually she began to unwind completely in the depths of the warm, scented water. She was refusing to let Adam Tudor into her head. Unable to see into his tricky mind, she couldn't begin to guess what he wanted with Martin and she had done all she could to keep him in ignorance of her uncle's whereabouts and, besides, everything would be all right, wouldn't it?

Almost an hour later she dragged herself out of the rapidly cooling water and slowly towelled herself dry. Taking her short-length, pale lemon silky wrap from the back of the bathroom door, she shrugged it on and tied the belt around her narrow waist, dragging her tawny mane of hair from beneath the collarless neckline. She would have one more try to contact Dominic and then go to bed and forget about the whole complicated mess. Tomorrow, bright and early, would be soon enough to resolve the problem of what to do about that troublesome man.

But Adam Tudor had other ideas and when she opened her bedroom door and found the troublesome man lying stretched out on her bed all hopes of a restful night scurried out of existence as every muscle in her body bunched up in outraged fury.

'You took your time.' Dark green eyes made a lazy assessment of her body as she simmered impotently with the embarrassing knowledge that the thin silky material was clinging too lovingly to every damp curve and hollow, that the wrap left far too much of her long naked legs on view and that he was enjoying every moment of his much too intimate scrutiny.

Her bare toes curled in a reflex of anguish into the deep pile of the carpet and her soft lips dragged back against her teeth as she instinctively snapped, 'What the hell do you think you're doing here?'

'Waiting for you. As I said, you took your time.' Sheer masculine sensuality lapped his lips as his half-hooded eyes lingered on the provocative line of her cleavage. 'But it was worth every second.'

Despite everything—what she knew of herself and of him—her mouth went dry, her heart punching against her ribs as she fought the crazy need to move closer to him. She wasn't into self-destruction yet the temptation to move into touching distance was agonisingly strong.

His long, hard body was stretched out on her bed, his lithe masculine potency making a mockery of its narrow virginity. One arm was flung above his head, his hand a relaxed curve, and he'd removed his tie, his jacket, and his shirt was open at the throat, the whiteness of the crisp fabric contrasting with the olive tones of his skin, making it darker, tempting... And Selina was tempted, tempted almost beyond endurance to touch, to discover whether that skin was as sleek and warm to touch as she imagined it to be...

'Get out!' The degree of violence in her voice was a direct reaction to her disgust with her own hitherto unsuspected sensuality, and perhaps he sensed that, she decided disgustedly, because those sexy eyes were light with laughter as he swung his long, hard-muscled, black-clad legs off the side of the bed, patted the vacant space at his side and said, in that bone-weakening voice,

'Nope. Come and join me, sweetheart. That mausoleum you put me in is too damned sombre for what I have in mind.'

She didn't need to ask what that might be; it was there in those sexy green eyes, in the subtle softening of that destructive mouth, so she wasn't going to give him the satisfaction of asking. And to stop herself from doing just that she punched out toughly, 'How did you know which was my room? A lucky guess? Or did you poke your nose behind every door in the house?'

He shook his head slowly, a 'more in sorrow than in anger' gesture that made her want to hit him, but his eyes were dancing as he stroked one lean-fingered hand over his jawline where the dark shadow of stubble was already beginning to show, and his voice was a drawl as he answered, 'I knew exactly where you sleep, I know your tastes in music, in food, I know how you like to spend your leisure time. You're crazy about Enya, Vivaldi and Gluck. You have a healthy appetite, will eat almost anything but prefer Italian food, and you like to walk. You got into that habit when you had a dog. A red setter, wasn't it? In fact, sweetheart, I know almost everything about you——' his grin was openly tigerish now and fear was a taste on her tongue '—and what I don't know already I am going to find out. I'm looking forward to that exercise immensely.'

Selina felt her body go cold. It was as if fear and disgust had frozen the blood in her veins. She tried not to shiver, to let him know just how frightened she was. It was as if an intruder had walked into her space, violating her most private possessions. And he was clever enough to know that, to take the advantage it gave him. And as much to fool him as to boost her own diminished courage she ground out, 'If you're not out of this room in one second, and out of the house in ten, I'm calling the police,' and lifted her chin defiantly to show him she meant exactly what she said and felt the breath coagulate in her lungs as his magnificent eyes caught and held hers, his voice a low, growly pussy-cat purr as he told her,

'I won't stop you, sweetheart. But you might find yourself on the wrong end of a whole load of embarrassing questions. I've every right to be here, you see. I own the damn place, lock, stock and bloody barrel.'

And she knew then just what those haunting, uneasy premonitions had been about. And her face went deathly white.

CHAPTER FOUR

'I DON'T believe you,' Selina managed at last, her voice dull. She was beginning to get a throbbing headache and her legs felt unsteady. She wondered if she was going to faint.

And he answered quietly, 'You mean you'd prefer not to.'

She shook her head, wincing as sudden pain stabbed unexpectedly behind her eyes, and his voice came gently, sounding a long way away. 'Sit down. It's time we talked.' His hands held hers, his grasp tightening just briefly before his palms slid upwards over the suddenly unbearably sensitised skin of her arms until they reached her shoulders. And that, and nothing else, was all she was aware of. Every heartbeat, every breath, every last cell of her body concentrated on the slow movements of his hands. And one of his hands slid beneath her arm and the other travelled so gently, so lightly down her body, just grazing the warm and rounded globes of her breasts, down over her ribcage to the soft swell of her stomach, on and on until it reached her thighs.

There was no anger, no justifiable outrage, simply that intense concentration, the single-minded homing-in of her senses to the brush of his hand against her body.

And then he scooped her in his arms and within moments she was sitting, as he had suggested. On the bed. Predictably.

Blaming her lack of resistance on shock, she tweaked the straying edges of the silky robe together and placed her bare feet primly side by side as she attempted to gather her woolly wits together.

Of course he didn't own Lower Otterley Hall and everything in it! His assertion had been complete nonsense, she chided herself as she felt the mattress dip when he sat beside her. He was playing games again and this time he'd gone too far.

'Go away,' she managed throatily, inwardly appalled by the utter ineptness of her retort, and couldn't have moved to save her life as his big body leaned over hers, a strong forefinger tilting her chin the better to gaze into her wide golden eyes.

'Poor baby,' he murmured, his voice a dangerous caress as his hand moved to curve around the slender stalk of her neck. 'You're cold and in shock.'

Running contrary to all her worst expectations, he moved away then, levering himself up from the bed and pulling the feather duvet around her, lapping her in immediate warmth. And, unable to look away, her shock-filled eyes followed his every movement as he walked to the centre of the room then turned, his feet planted apart, his thumbs hooked in his trouser pockets, pulling the dark fabric tautly across the flat narrowness of his hips. And if she hadn't known better she would have sworn there was compassion in those sexy green eyes as he told her, 'It's a case of overkill, I'm afraid, sweetheart. It's no contest, and that's a pity because I enjoy a fight.'

His lips lifted tauntingly and Selina came out of shock at his patronising, if incomprehensible words. She instinctively stiffened her spine, her chin jerking up, and her narrowed eyes took in the immediate answering gleam of response in his. And then her stomach gave a peculiar lurch as he drily informed her, 'I've come to the conclusion it's time I married. I'm thirty-seven years old and if I stopped working tomorrow I could live like a prince for the rest of my life. I've done virtually everything I've ever wanted to do and it's time I settled down.'

'Oh, bully for you!' Selina sniped, stung into reaction by his taunts about 'no contest'. Her wits had reassembled themselves, coming back from the outer edges of limbo where his outrageous assertion of his ownership of the Hall had scattered them. She gathered the bulky duvet more closely around her, fixed him with her long-lashed eyes and asked with sweet sarcasm, 'And who is the lucky lady?'

And he did it again. Blanked out her brain with the sheer force of outrageous shock tactics, leaving her to struggle out of the morass of blind panic as he told her calmly, 'Why, you are, sweetheart. Who else?' And walked out, closing the door gently behind him.

That night Selina discovered that one didn't have to be asleep to have nightmares.

Her first conclusion that Adam Tudor was insane was quickly but reluctantly discounted. He was far from off his trolley. He was determined, devious, and dangerous. It would have been more comforting if she could have marked him down as crazy.

After she'd pulled herself together, phoned the apartment where Dominic still wasn't answering, she tried to put the facts together in her head. Thinking clearly and concisely about events would be the only way to counter his questionable motives and methods.

Begin at the beginning, or what you know of it, she told herself as she crouched against the pillows, the duvet a smother of down around her tense body.

His absurd assertion about marrying her was thrust unceremoniously out of her head. No one could make her marry against her will.

And the beginning was, as she had been told, the situation of his birth.

As a young and inexperienced man, almost forty years ago, Martin had had an ill-considered encounter with an older, far more experienced woman. That much Dom had told her, and she had no reason, in the circumstances and taking into account Vanessa's reaction, to disbelieve it. So Adam had been conceived and born and, probably, his mother had wanted to marry Martin. But presumably he'd had more sense than that and had opted instead to support the two of them. And, by all accounts, Adam's mother had tried to soak Martin dry, over the years. That she had failed was self-evident, but she had continued to try. And after her death Adam had done the same—was still trying to do the same?

Selina wrinkled her brow, doing her best to think logically. Why had Martin had an attack when he'd read the message she'd left? Why had Dominic called Adam Tudor his father's enemy? And why had Vanessa said he was a greedy wretch and warned her that he could turn nasty?

It wasn't because Adam Tudor was threatening to tell anyone who might be interested that he was Martin's son. There could be no possible financial leverage in that. The circumstances of his birth might be regrettable but Vanessa and Dominic knew that much already, and these days there was no stigma about having an illegitimate offspring, especially as Martin had conscientiously taken care of both mother and child all down the years.

So there had to be far more to it than that.

But what? What hold did Adam Tudor have over his natural father? Why did he hate him to the point of bitter enmity? And why had he made that patently untrue claim to ownership of the Hall? None of it made the remotest sense!

And why, at a time when she'd been clearly thrown off balance, had he made that bad joke about marrying her? Why bring the subject of marriage up at all?

Selina wriggled out of the duvet and propped herself on one elbow. She stared at the bedside clock with consternation. After lying awake all night she'd dropped off to sleep when it was time to get up and now it was gone ten. Typical of the way her luck seemed to be running just now!

Pushing a mass of tawny curls out of her eyes, she reached for the phone, but Dominic's secretary said, 'He's not here. He came in yesterday and left with a bunch of papers after about ten minutes. He said to expect him back when we saw him. I was so sorry to hear about Mr King; how is he progressing?'

'We're keeping our fingers crossed he'll be all right.' Martin was the first of Selina's worries and due to all that aggro with Adam Tudor last night she'd completely forgotten to contact Vanessa and enquire how he was. It made her feel guilty. But she was, she tried to console herself, doing her best on his behalf, trying to discover what his elder son was up to. Though up to now it had been a pretty poor best, she recognised dully. 'And Dominic didn't say where he'd be?' she pressed, pushing unproductive thoughts aside.

'No, but I assumed he'd be at Lower Otterley to be near the hospital and his father.' His secretary sounded surprised, as well she might, Selina thought drily as she ended the conversation with a few pleasantries then quickly punched in the numbers of the London apartment.

He'd obviously been there at some time during the night because now the answering machine was operational and she left a message, asking him to contact her urgently, then scrambled out of bed.

Dominic was probably on his way here right now, she told herself as she hurriedly dressed in a pair of well-worn olive-green cords and a thick Aran sweater. Unless he'd heard a weather forecast and decided not to risk it, the voice of reason prodded. But, in that case, where the hell was he?

Not that it really mattered, of course. She and her cousin had never been close but it would have been nice to have some back-up if the unpredictable Adam Tudor became harder to handle than he already was.

She could hardly hope that he, too, had overslept, and wondering what he was doing had her scampering down the back staircase to the kitchen, where Meg had just finished washing the floor. And before the housekeeper could get an insulting remark in about hard nights and the need to catch up on much needed sleep she asked coolly, 'Has Mr Tudor surfaced yet?' hoping she sounded indifferent.

'Hours ago.' Meg leant on the mop handle. 'If you want breakfast you'd better make it yourself; I've got a busy day ahead.'

Hours ago. So what was he up to now? Selina wondered about putting the kettle on for a much wanted pot of tea then scuppered the idea. Heaven only knew what Tudor was doing. According to Meg he'd had the free run of the house for hours. She didn't trust him an inch. And she turned to the door but Meg was saying, 'He came down the same time as me. And while I made breakfast he cleared the grates. And brought in fresh fuel without me so much as dropping a hint.'

He had obviously found favour in that quarter. Selina swallowed the acid comment that was just bursting to drop off her tongue and enquired, idly, she hoped, 'So what's he doing now?'

'He's gone.' Meg took the mop and bucket through to the utility-room and came back wiping her hands on her flowered apron. And Selina, heaving a sigh of relief because luck had turned in her favour at last, went to put the kettle on for that tea. But she asked, suspicion tinging her voice because his leaving without her having to summon the SAS to throw him out seemed almost too good to be true,

'Gone? How? I thought we were snowed in.'

'Too true. If you're making tea, I'll have a cup. But it seems it turned to rain in the night. Not that it's clear yet. I thought it still looked too dodgy for him to take his car out, but he didn't listen. Something upset him. He was happy as Larry one minute, enjoying his bacon and eggs, chatting away as if he'd known me for years.' She took the teacup Selina gave her and sat down at the table, apparently forgetting about the busy day ahead of her, and apart from raising one eyebrow Selina didn't comment because she was too busy wondering what had got under Tudor's skin to such an extent.

It had to be something Meg had said. So she took her cup and joined the other woman at the table, and sure enough Meg explained it all, and when she had Selina wished she hadn't.

'He was saying what a beautiful house this is and I was agreeing, telling him about what's known of its history, then I told him we were all under a bit of a cloud

at the moment, on account of Mr King's heart attack.'
Meg stirred her tea and Selina pushed hers away.

Martin's illness was the very last thing that monster
should have learned about. And it was all her fault! If
she hadn't fallen asleep just when she should have been
getting up she would have been in time to warn the
housekeeper to say nothing on that subject, just as she'd
planned to do last night! And Meg was saying—although
Selina didn't have to be told because she could guess
exactly what had happened next—'He asked where Mr
King was now, and I told him, and he just stood up from
the table—left a good half of his breakfast—and went.'

'Quite a time ago, you said?' Selina made the question
casual but her heart was racing fit to leap out of her
body and the sight of the tea in her cup made her feel
ill. And she didn't even have the relief of bawling Meg
out for giving the information because Meg would only
feel guilty and the guilt wasn't hers. She, Selina, should
have made sure she warned the housekeeper. This latest,
monstrous twist in the game Tudor was playing was due
to her own inexcusable negligence.

And over Meg's reply of, 'Oh, about an hour ago, I'd
say,' she got to her feet and hurried back up the stairs
to her room. He'd had plenty of time to get to the hospital, get to Martin, but she hoped, oh, how she hoped,
that he'd come to grief on the slithery, slushy roads and
ended up in a ditch. But knowing him, having experienced first hand the sense of invicible power and purpose
that came off him in waves, she didn't doubt that he'd
achieved just what he'd set out to do.

And in this she was proved right as she phoned through
to the hospital and spoke to Vanessa in the room she
was using in the private wing.

'Yes, he's been,' Vanessa answered her blurted question with quiet bitterness. 'He got in by telling the nursing officer he was Martin's son. I was in the bathroom at the time or he wouldn't have got his nose round the door.' Selina heard her aunt pull in a deep breath, her voice harder as she castigated, 'How could you have told him where Martin was? How could you? I took you in because you were my only sister's child—gave you every advantage in life—and this is how you repay me!'

'Believe me, it wasn't intentional.' Now wasn't the time to go into the whys and wherefores. 'How's Martin? Is Adam Tudor still with him?' She had to know what had happened, how Martin had taken the surprise visitation from the man Dominic had said was his enemy.

And Vanessa said flatly, as if her outburst had drained her of energy, 'He left a few minutes ago. And Martin seems—seems OK.'

'Not upset?' Selina expelled a sigh of relief. She didn't think she was strong enough to carry the load of guilt if her negligence had resulted in a set-back, or worse, to her uncle's health.

'Not so you'd notice.' The hard tone was back, but with a faint, underlying wobble that Selina could sympathise with. Her aunt had been through so much anxiety recently that she must have seen Adam Tudor as the final straw. 'Actually, he's been asking to see you. It was the first thing he said when I went into his room after that creature left.'

So Adam had spoken to Martin alone. At his insistence? Probably. What had he said or done to make the possessive and protective Vanessa comply? Aloud, she asked, 'Did Martin tell you what Adam wanted? Why it was so important that they talk?' Up to date, Vanessa

had never confided in her over anything she considered
to be really important. It was her aunt's way of making
sure Selina never forgot that, though she'd always been
made welcome, always been cared for, she was not, and
never could be, a full member of the tightly knit family
of three. And she wasn't confiding now.

'No.' The negative was explosive with bitterness and
Selina wondered if it was the truth, if Martin hadn't told
her what his first-born, illegitimate son had wanted. It
was a thought to be conjured with. 'There's something
I want you to do for me,' Vanessa was going on, and
Selina assented on a rush, still feeling guilty about the
way Adam had discovered Martin's whereabouts,

'I'll do anything I can; you know that.'

'Fetch Dominic back. I want him here. He's at the
apartment.'

'I know.' At least she assumed he must be there. 'I
left a message on the answering machine, telling him to
contact me urgently. I'll wait for his call and then tell
him you want him.'

'No. Go up to town and fetch him back.' Vanessa
sounded beyond patience. 'I've left messages, too. But
he's probably shut himself up with his work, refusing
to take calls, or listen to messages. You know how involved he gets, how his responsibilities come first.'

Selina knew nothing of the kind. Vanessa had always
been blinkered where her only, precious offspring was
concerned, seeing only what she wanted to see. But, because her aunt had been through a lot just recently, she
said soothingly, 'Of course I'll drive up. I'll see you this
evening when I visit Martin and I'll do my best to bring
Dominic with me.'

The trip to town wasn't one she was overjoyed to be
making, Selina thought as she pulled a soft leather jacket

out of her wardrobe and pushed her feet into warm, fur-lined boots. Once off the country lanes the road conditions would be better, she consoled herself, but even so she was sure she was setting out on a wild-goose chase.

She rang the apartment again and was connected to the answering machine. Vanessa's theory tied up with the information that Dominic had taken papers away from the office but it still didn't make sense. He knew his father's condition was precarious. Even though the attack had been minor these first few days were critical. And, that being the case, why should he refuse to answer his phone, not even bothering to listen to messages?

Besides, he had known Adam Tudor had been meeting with her last night. So why hadn't he phoned home to find out what had transpired, asked about his father's health? He seemed to have disappeared off the face of the earth.

The questions wriggled through her head during the next hour, and no one was answering. The fruitless questioning, the concentration needed on the poor road conditions left the inside of her skull feeling as if it was lined with broken glass, and she was relieved, if not too hopeful, when she parked the Volvo on the relatively quiet street off Earl's Court and made her way to the converted apartment block.

The moment she stepped inside the flat she knew she was alone. The central heating was turned down low, just enough warmth to keep the place aired, keep the pipes from freezing. And the place had the forlorn and musty atmosphere it always had when no one had used it for a while.

Shivering, she went through to the sitting-room and switched on the electric fire. Then she listened to the messages on the machine. Her voice and, predictably, Vanessa's.

Her strongly arched brows drawn down over her long eyes, Selina went through to the kitchen. She had missed breakfast entirely and needed coffee before she could even begin to think things through. The fridge was unplugged, the door open, as they always left it when the flat was not in use, and while the kettle boiled she poked her head in the two bedrooms. Neither the double bed nor the two singles had been made up, let alone slept in.

Dominic had come here, briefly, to activate the answering machine. And then he had gone. Where? And why?

After pouring boiling water on to the coffee granules, she took her mug through to the sitting-room and cradled it in her hands, staring at the glowing bars of the fire.

Nothing to get in a panic about, of course. It was puzzling but there was probably a perfectly acceptable answer. Maybe he'd set out lateish last night, run into that snowstorm and decided to sit it out in some roadside inn. He was probably back at Lower Otterley right now. He was probably——

She heard the key in the lock and the sound of the door closing heavily back into its frame and she swung round, putting her coffee down on the low table in front of the hearth.

Dominic. Her golden eyes glinted with a mixture of relief and irritation. She'd skin him alive! Just because he hadn't been bothered to get in touch with anyone, she'd been sent to check up on him, wasting time when she could have been visiting Martin, maybe even finding out what the devil Adam Tudor had wanted of him.

And talk of the devil he was there, shouldering his way through into the sitting-room, filling the door-frame, his face a tough, mind-blanking mask of fury as he bit out, 'Where is he?' His eyes were glittering shards of emerald, set in the hewn granite of his memorable features. 'Don't bother, I'll look.' He strode towards the open kitchen door, flinging over his shoulder, 'Just don't say a word. Not one,' he ground out, slewing round to face her as she flung a howl of outrage after him. 'I'm just about mad enough to shake the life out of you, so don't forget it.' For a moment his lips were drawn back against his teeth and then his fury exploded in shattering condemnation. 'How dare you keep the truth of my father's condition from me? He could have been dying, and I wouldn't have known. How dare you?'

Sheer bewilderment caught at her throat and it was still reflected in her eyes when he marched back into the room after the few moments it had taken him to search the entire flat.

If he truly cared for his father, then his anger would be perfectly understandable. But she knew the reverse was the case. As far as she knew, he was his father's enemy. The note announcing his imminent arrival had been responsible for Martin's heart attack... And yet, according to Vanessa, the elderly man hadn't been in the least upset by that visit to the hospital...

It was an unreal situation and, facing the blazing anger of his narrowed green eyes, she grasped at the only tangible thought and demanded, 'What do you mean by barging in here? And who the hell gave you a key?'

He stared at her as if he had never seen her before and said harshly, 'Where is he? Typical of Dominic King to hide behind a woman's skirts. His mother's made sure he knows how. But it won't do him a scrap of good. So tell me where he is. Now!'

Selina swallowed hard. There was far more to this nightmare than she'd thought. She knew it in her bones. But if Adam Tudor thought he could browbeat her he could think again. He was big, he was menacing, he was dangerous. But she had more guts than he obviously gave her credit for and although her golden eyes were stormy her voice was clear and cool as she countered, 'You didn't answer my question. I said——'

'I know what you said,' he cut across her voice, emphasising the interruption with a downward slash of his hand. And his own voice was as cool as hers, anger sliding out of it but still alive, lodged behind his eyes. 'And I can guarantee you won't like the answer. I own this flat, just as I own the Hall and the controlling interest in the King's Ransom chain.' He jerked a thumb over his shoulder, towards the telephone on a corner table. 'If you're not prepared to take my word for it, phone Martin. Ask him.' And then the cutting edge of sheer fury was back again, his mouth tight as he lashed out, 'Why the hell didn't you tell me he was ill?'

It was all too much to take in. Had he been telling the truth last night when he'd said he owned the Hall and everything in it? The way Selina mentally dismissed his bitter suggestion that she could corroborate his story with her uncle gave her back her answer and she felt for the fireside chair with the back of her knees and sat down with a bump——

And lifted her long, shock-hazed eyes to find him standing over her, his sheepskin unbuttoned, his hands firm on his narrow hips. 'Well? I could kill you for pussyfooting around, playing games, when all the time you knew my father was desperately ill!'

He was acting as if he cared and she shook her head to clear it, a frown darkening her eyes to amber. She moistened her lips, her spirit surging back after the rough blow he'd dealt it, met the scathing contempt in his eyes and said with tart sweetness, 'You may have somehow stolen Martin's property and half his business, or blackmailed him out of everything he's ever worked for, but you don't frighten me. I don't tell you anything I don't want to tell you. Now, or ever.' Wild rose colour stained the surface of her normally creamy skin and she met his narrowed, glinting eyes without flinching, and heard him suck in his breath, saw the violent pulse-beat of his anger at the side of his jaw and knew he would have attacked her physically had he been a weaker kind of man.

As it was, no bodily harm could have been worse than his coldly intoned, 'If you want to bring blackmail into the conversation, try this on for size: I am in a position to ruin Martin and see Dominic behind bars. And this I will most assuredly do unless you agree to be my wife.'

CHAPTER FIVE

'How stupid can you get?' Selina shot back at him immediately. And then her bones began to quake as she recognised that what he'd said hadn't been just a bad joke, not as far as he was concerned.

There was a look of damning purpose in his eyes, a hardness, glittering points of pure emerald light that scorched her with cold dislike. She had always known there was a mind like a steel trap behind the façade of devastating charm he had seemed able to turn on at will.

Suddenly, uncontrollably, she began to shiver.

She heard the harsh rasp of his breath and found his eyes on a level with hers as he squatted down in front of her, and that sexy voice was a caress of heavy rough velvet as he put her discarded mug of coffee in her hands and told her, 'Drink this. It might help. And then we'll get out of this gloomy hole. There's a lot we have to get sorted out.'

The flat wasn't gloomy and it wasn't a hole. When one or two of the family were staying in town it could be quite cosy. And it was convenient for the office.

Her mind fixed on her defence of the small, four-roomed flat because it stopped her from thinking about his last statement. She didn't want to have to listen to his method of sorting things out, and she didn't want the coffee either. If she managed to get a single drop past the tight constriction in her throat, her churning stomach would reject it at once.

She put the mug down on the floor, unconsciously shaking her head, and Adam gave her a look of jerky exasperation before rising to his feet, taking her hands and pulling her with him.

And her skin shouldn't burn beneath the grip of those strong, beautifully shaped hands, and the warmth of his handclasp shouldn't be sending shock waves through her system. And slowly, against all conscious thought, her long-lashed, slumbrous golden eyes drifted upwards to linger on his mouth, and fastened there, her heart jerking within her breast as she saw the finely chiselled lips soften with the ghost of a flickering, knowing smile.

The need, the aching, aching desire to have him kiss her again shocked her, jolted her out of the unreality of the situation, the fantasy, the illusion of the sensation of bonding... It was impossible, unworthy of her, and she dragged her hands out of his and wrapped her arms around her body. Then Adam said forcefully, 'Let's go.'

She should have snapped out a refusal, or, at the very least, demanded to know what he had in mind. But her brain was scrambled, numbed by that momentary aberration back there, and she could only watch blankly as he switched off the fire, unable to do more than allow herself to be herded out and into his gun-metal-grey, top-of-the-range Mercedes.

Only after he'd pulled out into the traffic could she manage, 'What do you think you're doing?' and that shakily, her voice lacking commitment.

'Taking you to my home, where we can relax and talk.' He cut into a hurtling flow of traffic with a panache that didn't entirely surprise her and he was brain-dead if he thought she could ever relax with him. Around him she was as jumpy as a cat on hot coals. 'There's a lot to be discussed so we might as well begin right now. So I'll ask again: where is Dominic skulking?'

'I've no idea.'

It was puzzling her, too, and her brows were drawn together in a frown as he gave her a darting, sideways glance and said tightly, 'I'd be inclined to believe you. From what I know of you, you wouldn't turn a blind eye to what he's been doing. But I can't forget the way you played your damned games with me when you knew where Martin was, how ill he was.'

So what had Dominic been doing? Somehow that didn't seem so important at the moment. She was getting herself together at last, making plans. As soon as they reached his home, wherever, she would be off like a shot, grabbing a taxi to take her back to her own car. She had her cheque-book and purse in the handbag clasped on her lap, her fingernails biting into the soft leather.

Yet his implication that she might somehow be bound up with whatever he believed Dom to be doing—and he'd made it sound nefarious, hadn't he just?—got her on the raw. And he didn't know a single thing about her, about the real Selina Roth, and that was all entwined with her vehement words, 'I love my uncle! When he learned you intended to visit he had a heart attack—that's how overjoyed he was at the news! So do you wonder why I did my best to keep you from knowing where he was, pestering him?'

She glared across at him, furious at the slight smile she saw on that otherwise impervious profile. 'Dom told me you were his enemy, and he was right. Dead right if what you've told me about your taking everything he owns away from him is true. And you can stop making judgements about what I might or might not do where my cousin is concerned because despite what you said you don't know me at all. You can't even begin to!'

'Don't you believe it.' His voice raised goose-bumps on her skin. 'How do you imagine I knew your tastes in food and music? How I knew about your dog? Martin gave him to you as a puppy on your fourteenth birthday. You were heartbroken when he died last year. You called him Sam.'

She had forgotten he had all kinds of personal knowledge about her. At least, she had shoved it to the back of her mind because other things had taken precedence. But now it all came jolting back, the feelings of violation, the shuddery sensation that an intruder was walking around inside her life.

'I'll tell you, since you can't bring yourself to ask,' he remarked into her tight, defensive silence, turning the car away from the Thames. 'Over the years, Martin has spoken about you. Singing your praises. To me. Through him I've got to know so much. He couldn't have loved you more if you'd been his own flesh and blood.'

Selina closed her eyes against a sudden wash of tears. She'd always known Martin loved her far more than Vanessa, her own blood-relative, had. His care for her, his concern that the bewildered orphan should know that she had a second family rooting for her, cherishing her, had been the only thing that had made the sudden and devastating loss of both parents possible to bear.

She supposed she would never know what madness had prompted him to talk about her to Adam—over the years, he had said, which meant that the relationship between father and son had not been cut off when he'd come of age, as Vanessa had implied.

But one thing was becoming horribly clear. Adam knew how fond of her Martin was, how he thought of her as his own daughter. His threat to blackmail her into marriage was beginning to make a twisted kind of sense. By doing so he would take her away from Martin, too, just as he had taken his home and his business. He knew how devastated Martin would feel if he saw his adopted daughter tied in a loveless marriage to his enemy.

As Adam turned the Mercedes into a mews, a stone's throw from the river, she stopped chewing the corner of her bottom lip and changed her mind about making a run for it. Things were not as clear-cut black and white as she'd believed them to be. Were they ever?

He parked the car on the cobbles in front of a rosy brick cottage and her eyes fixed on the tubs of winter-flowering cyclamens that flanked the glossy hardwood main door, not really seeing them.

He had been presented to her as Martin's enemy and his threat to ruin his own father and half-brother had been a savage endorsement of that. And his threat to blackmail her into marriage was, quite obviously, an un-subtle form of revenge.

He was possessed of enviable looks and the type of charisma which, though indefinable, was impossible to ignore. And he hadn't been at the back of the queue in the brains department, either. So what had cut so deeply into his psyche? What had made him turn his back on his natural advantages and cling doggedly to his need for power and revenge?

Was it because, as he saw it, he had been rejected by his father as a child? Was that the poisonous root of the problem?

There was only one way to find out.

And perhaps, when she'd discovered what drove him, she could do something about it.

Not questioning her reluctance to tell him to go to hell and do his worst, she waited in thoughtful silence as he walked round the front of the car to help her out. But she was on her feet before he could touch her and that made good sense because when he touched her her body reacted instinctively, the chemistry between them blinding her to all logic and reason.

The room he took her into was panelled with smooth old oak, warm, furnished functionally with an entirely masculine disregard for unnecessary detail. He shrugged out of his sheepskin then held out a hand for her leather jacket, but Selina shook her head, stuffing her hands in her pockets, binding the garment around her.

'Have you eaten?' His eyes watched her with bland serenity, as if he knew she was using her coat as armour, wary of relinquishing anything to him. And again she shook her head, then summoned her voice.

'I'm not hungry.'

'Coffee, then.' And that wasn't a question. She watched narrowly as he strode softly from the room, her eyes pinned to the elegant, quite beautiful male symmetry of him. Alone, she dragged in her breath and compressed her lips firmly. The spell that man cast was dark, primeval. He wove it, enmeshing her, without even trying. She had to fight it. Above all, she had to do that.

And she could. She would.

Walking to an oblong mirror, framed in dull antique gilt, she noted with a kind of horror that her wide mouth was parted with a soft vulnerability, her long eyes more slumbrous than ever before, dreamy. And that wasn't the way she mentally saw herself at all.

Again, Selina compressed her lips and made sure they stayed that way as she dragged her fingers through the riot of her tawny, gold-streaked hair, a tumbled tousle that, as ever, stubbornly resisted all her attempts to subdue it. She then turned quickly as she heard his approach, not panicking but determined he should not discover her there, in front of the mirror. His ego was massive enough to let him believe she was prinking for him.

He was carrying a tray and he put it down on a small Pembroke table; while he was pouring from the filter jug she straightened her spine and asked levelly, 'So what's all this about, Adam? You've obviously got a grudge against Martin and his entire family. You tell me you're in a position to ruin him—and I'll believe that because unless and until I get evidence to tell me you're lying I have to—so what I want to know is, why?'

She saw the wide shoulders stiffen, his whole body going still for a second before he resumed his task, and his voice held a hint of self-derision as he told her, 'It's a long story.'

'We've got all day,' she pointed out, her mind looking on with stoic amazement at the vagaries of her tongue. She didn't want to spend time with him; the less she saw of him the safer she would be. Turning, he gave a tight, almost feral smile, a smile that didn't touch his eyes, and, more than ever, she regretted her earlier statement—especially so when he drawled, making her hackles rise,

'Point taken. But I can think of far better ways of spending the time.'

Selina ignored that comment; it was the only thing to do. She took the cup he held out to her and carried it over to the far side of the hearth, taking a much needed moment to pretend interest in a small, framed watercolour of a stone cottage in a high, mountainous valley before perching on the edge of a chocolate linen-covered winged armchair. If he hadn't come up with any answers by the time she'd finished her coffee, she would leave, she promised herself. And if he so much as mentioned marriage again she would hit him!

But when he asked softly, 'Do you have any deep-rooted objections to the state of matrimony? I don't think you're planning on entering a nunnery. According to Martin, you've had boys flocking around you since you were sixteen,' she merely closed her eyes and gritted her teeth and gripped her saucer until the coffee-cup rattled.

'So?' she managed through tight lips, sweeping her lashes up to give him a pugnacious stare.

What on earth had prompted her uncle to give this devil a blow-by-blow account of her life with her adoptive family? Yes, she'd had her fair share of boyfriends, but never anything serious. She'd been too single-minded about carving out a place for herself, establishing her own individual identity, to make time for any long-term emotional commitments. But, the thought came from nowhere, shocking her by its implications, the emphasis had been on boyfriends. Maybe her emotions had remained untouched, untouchable, simply because she had never come up against a real man before. And Adam Tudor was more man than most.

She flinched, and he rubbed salt in the wound.

'So you haven't taken vows of celibacy and neither have I. And, as I told you, it's time I married. And as you're in no position to turn me down I think it's time we made plans.'

He had lit the coal-effect gas fire and was straddling the hearth, his back to it, drinking his coffee.

Selina put her own cup aside before she gave in to the impulse to hurl the scalding contents in his face. She stood up quickly, her stormy eyes scathing as she bit out, 'I'm going. If you can't talk sense I'm not listening.'

But his silky voice stopped her. 'Does a million and a half make sense? Pounds sterling. Can you brush that aside so lightly?' And she turned then, because she had to, and met the cold intensity of his eyes and admitted that for once she was way out of her league.

He wasn't to know that, though. Wasn't to know that her spine was crawling with dread. And she said, her voice sounding thin, drowned out by the drum-beats of her heart, 'I don't know what you're talking about.'

'No?' His mouth twisted wryly. 'You're lying.'

Exasperated, Selina searched the cold green depths of his eyes, and found nothing but a flicker of contempt that fanned her own anger. She bit down hard on her lower lip. Raging at him would get her nowhere, nowhere but deeper and deeper into the mire of confusion he had created.

Dragging air deep into her lungs, she repeated, 'I don't know what you mean. And I don't lie.'

'Or only when it suits you.' He put his cup down on the hearth and walked towards her, making her heart stand still and then race on. 'You lied about Martin. Why should I believe anything you say?'

'I told you why!' She wouldn't back down; she couldn't afford to. 'Why should I lie about anything else?'

For a moment, just a heartbeat of time, she saw doubt deep in his eyes before they iced over again, then melted, the long, gold-tipped dark lashes almost meeting over a glimmer of green as his mouth curved tauntingly.

'Either way, it's not the end of the world. Sainthood is not what I'm looking for in a wife.' His eyes drifted over her flushed features, his voice lowering to that inimicable, husky caress. 'I require spirit, and you have that in abundance; I demand fidelity, loyalty, and shall exact both.' His wide shoulders lifted in a minimal shrug, the green gleam of his eyes sharpened with cynicism. 'I can take the odd white lie as long as I learn how to recognise it. And I shall; believe me, I shall.'

'What reason would I have for marrying you?' She shrugged his words away, playing for time, her mind wallowing in the fog of confusion he had created.

But he came back smoothly, 'Reasons? Roughly a million and a half of them, I'd say.' He made a sweeping movement with one hand, gesturing towards the chair she had so abruptly vacated. 'Sit down, and I'll spell them out for you.'

'I prefer to stand.' She stood her ground, refusing to give an inch, then wished she'd done as he'd suggested when he walked towards her, planting his supple body a scant inch away from hers. And the room was suddenly far too warm, her body flooding with heat beneath restricting clothing, and she took a defensive backward step and found his hands on her shoulders, his eyes pinning her to the spot.

'Stop trying to run,' he commanded softly, that rough velvet voice weakening her bones. 'You can't run far enough, or fast enough. Believe that, and we'll begin to make progress.' His strong fingers were moulding the bones of her shoulders beneath the soft leather and wool and she tried to lunge out of his reach because any physical contact with him was dangerous and she could feel the danger already in the quickening of her senses, the excited clamour of her heartbeats.

But he was ready for her, conceding nothing, his arms effortlessly scooping her off her feet and planting her down on the sofa flanking the other side of the hearth.

He came down beside her, all in one fluid movement, his arms still a prison around her heated body. Thick black lashes screened a blaze of emerald-green, compelling her own slitted gaze. She felt mesmerised, held by the nameless raw chemistry that flushed his high, angular cheekbones, tightened his jaw and hazed the glitter of his eyes. Then, after a whisper of time, fraught with an emotion she couldn't categorise, his lips curled in a grim smile as he withdrew his arms and commanded, 'Sit.'

Just as if she were a troublesome dog, Selina thought raggedly, pushing herself unsteadily back into antagonism, away from the baited trap of that brief moment back there when something had seemed to explode into life between them.

'You want reasons, I'll give them to you.' His dark voice curled round a threat that made her want to run and hide. Instead, her fingers twisted together in her lap. He had already told her she couldn't run far or fast enough, and now she believed him. If she made so much as a tiny movement away from him he would haul her back, his hands, his body touching hers. At least, although he was sitting far too close for her peace of mind, he wasn't manhandling her, and she stared doggedly ahead, keeping her face blank, while her appalled mind struggled with what he was telling her.

'Twelve months ago Martin approached me in my professional capacity. The King's Ransom chain was beginning to be hit badly by the recession and he needed a large injection of cash. My bank made it available, but, naturally, we had to have collateral. We took the deeds of the Hall and the London flat and a sizeable number of shares. But surely you knew all that?'

She shook her head, not because she hadn't been told that the family business was in hock to one of the City's most prestigious merchant banks, but because she now knew why his name had rung bells.

She had once read an article in one of the financial papers about the young, dynamic high-flyer who had forced himself on to the board of one of the capital's oldest and stodgiest banks and had, almost single-handedly, wrestled it into its present position of power in the money world.

Adam Tudor. And he was Martin's son. Martin had gone to him for help and the bastard had taken the opportunity to get the father he believed had rejected him hopelessly into his power.

It was all beginning to make sense. Had he gone to the house on the evening of Martin's birthday to express the bank's intention of calling in the loan? Had Martin known that? Had that knowledge been responsible for his heart attack? It was the only logical conclusion. Yet why had Vanessa and Dominic been so sure he had come looking for charity, a massive hand-out that would ensure he could continue to maintain his chosen lifestyle? Didn't they know that Adam—and Adam Tudor was, to all intents and purposes, the bank—had the power and probably the desire to ruin them all?

Yet hadn't Dominic told her that Adam would like to see them in the bankruptcy courts? She furrowed her brow in concentration and Adam said on a whispery growl, 'Don't scowl. You'll get wrinkles.'

'So what's that to you?' A foolish, foolish thing to say. Her brain went into cold storage when he was around, she recognised with distraught regret as the tip of a forefinger smoothed away the frown-lines, moving in tiny lingering caresses along the arched silkiness of her eyebrows. Selina's eyes drifted shut, the lids languorously heavy with drifting response to the exquisite sensuality of his touch.

Sensing the slow movement of his head and shoulders, she made an abortive effort to open her eyes, to rid herself of the sultry sensation of drowning in warm honey, then felt his lips touch hers, laying their silken length against her own just softly, and a sensational explosion of something too delicious to be painful turned the pit of her stomach to liquid fire, making her gasp.

And, taking advantage, as he always would, he slid the tip of his tongue possessively between her parted lips, curling provocatively into the moist recesses, and someone groaned. Herself? Maybe. And he murmured against her mouth, his sexy voice unforgivably spiked with amusement, 'You are physical perfection. When you're my wife, I shall want you to stay that way.'

'Oooh!' Her whole body seemed to fry with the explosive implications of his words; she felt as if she was being sucked into a fiery whirlpool of molten lava. Yet he wasn't holding her, only his drugging lips were binding her; she only had to pull away.

She managed it, dismayed by the difficulty, the unreasoning regret, the lingering sensation of dizziness, and she husked, trying to banish the haze of aroused sensuality from the gold of her eyes, replace it with some of that old fire and fury, 'Will you stop talking of marriage? It's out of the question, and you know it. You're only doing it to torment me.' She risked a look, a doubtful one at that, and saw one black brow lilt upwards, the corners of his ravaging mouth quirk sideways.

'Out of the question? Why?' A whisper. A caress in itself.

She clamped her lips together to stop them opening in tempting invitation then sucked in her breath as he put a hand on her cord-trousered knee. The heat of it flayed her, the light pressure enough to send wicked, betraying heat clear up to the top of her thighs, curling insidiously between them. She gave a choked sob. Her response to him disgusted her.

She smacked his hand away and levered herself up from the semi-supine position her body had somehow got itself into and croaked at him, 'According to you, the bank you work for——' she deliberately denigrated his omnipotent position, revelling in her own spite because she had precious few other weapons '—staked King's Ransom when the going got tough. Demanded collateral—which is normal—and got it. Technically speaking, you could probably call in the loan and ruin us. Martin couldn't have read the small print, I guess. Though ruining us wouldn't do you much good. But that's your business.'

'Precisely.'

She had been staring straight ahead, not trusting herself to look at him, but the laid-back amusement of his tone had her glancing sideways, noting, with a snort of fury, the emerald flames that danced in the liquid depths of his wicked green eyes.

She had stupidly allowed him to seduce her senses away, making her forget just what a louse he was. Any man who could talk of blackmail, the ruination of a respected family business and the loss of scores of jobs, had to have a twisted mind.

Besides, surely there was something she could do to spike his guns?

The glimmer of returning confidence gave her the courage to turn and face him with a tiny, condescending smile, her voice nice and cool now as she hazarded, 'I'm sure there must be a watchdog organisation I could appeal to—some judicious body who oversees corporate deals, who can come down hard on creeps like you who attempt blackmail.'

'I'm sure you're right.' He had the audacity to grin and her stupid heart responded by missing a beat.

She collected herself sternly, grasping her new-found determination by the throat, telling him loftily, 'I know I am. However, I demand to see a copy of the contract Martin signed, to winkle out the pernicious small print. And then I will go to—er—whoever, and put my case.'

'Why not look on it as a private arrangement between the two of us?' A hand lifted to push back the tumble of tawny curls that had fallen forwards, hiding her face. His mouth was too close to hers, much too close, and her eyes fastened dazedly on his, unable to look away as he murmured, 'Why wash your dirty linen in public?'

'I haven't any,' she contradicted past the frantic pulse-beat in her throat, watching those thick black lashes sweep down to hide his eyes, minutely conscious of the way his fingertips still lingered on the silky fragrance of her hair.

'No, I don't suppose you have,' he said thickly. 'You're like a cute little engine, sitting on the tracks, with a full head of exuberant steam, but no one in the driver's seat. Aren't you too hot in this thing?' Both of his hands were on the collar of her soft leather jacket, but, not taking time to be aware of the fact, she accused,

'Are you trying to tell me I'm sixpence short of a shilling?' and felt the jacket slide away from her shoulders and was too put out by his denigrating comment to care. Besides, what with the central heating, the fire, her thick Aran sweater, she had been feeling much too warm...

'Not at all.' His voice was too soothing to be trusted, but his, 'On the contrary, I know you're very bright. Just under-utilised. With your talents you should be running the chain. Martin has very wisely taken a back seat, and Dominic simply hasn't got what it takes,' had her eyes batting open. Did he mean he wasn't out to bankrupt them after all? Did he enjoy talking in riddles?

'I don't understand.' He had taken off his suit jacket, tossing it over the arm of a chair. Absently, her gaze followed the movement. 'If you bankrupt us, there won't be a business to run.' She met the probing assessment of his remarkable eyes, vaguely registering that he was removing his tie. It joined his jacket. 'So this discussion is purely academic,' she pointed out huskily, and dragged her eyes away because he had opened the top two buttons of his shirt, exposing the taut column of his throat, giving a tantalising glimpse of the crisp dark hairs that lay against the oiled silk, olive-toned skin.

'Not necessarily. I have no real interest in seeing the King's Ransom chain go under.' He had angled himself into the corner of the sofa, his long legs stretched out so that one of his knees nudged one of hers. A wash of heat flared over her body and she curled her fingers into her palms, trying to clear her mind, to rid herself of the degrading desire to reach out and touch that exposed triangle of skin, to slide her hands beneath the fine white fabric of his shirt, to get to know the shape of him, the warmth, the strength, the silken sheathed hardness of him...

Her body went rigid in her frantic effort to find the self-control she had formerly possessed in abundance and she flinched wildly as the back of his fingers drifted caressingly over her clamped jawline.

'Relax.' He had moved closer, much closer, and his fingers turned, gently rubbing her lower lip now, and she gave a choked moan, hating herself for allowing this to happen, despising her lack of courage and will, and his dark head bent forward, his mouth taking over where his fingertips had opened the way, leaving his hand free to slide down her body, find the hem of her sweater and dip beneath.

At the touch of his firm, warm hand on the soft skin of her midriff the whole world stood still—— And then raced forwards on a wave of sensation that was shatteringly physical, and Selina had to struggle against the rip-tide of sensuality that made her head spin to make any sense at all out of what he was saying.

'At the moment, King's Ransom is doing fine. But the loan still has to be repaid.' His fingers walked upwards, hovering now beneath the lower curve of her swollen breasts, and desire, sweet and sharp, stabbed at her stomach, making her breath catch in her lungs. She tried to push his hand away, but there was no strength in her, not anywhere, and he added huskily, 'It can be done, eventually, given good management, good buying techniques—which, with your proven expertise and sound business sense, can be taken for granted. Given that, and given that Dominic stops milking the funds, and your agreement to our marriage, the boutiques will be on course to enjoy a roaring success.'

'Marriage'—that one word had her fighting to emerge from the treacherous ground of physical need. She shook her head, moistened her lips with the tip of her tongue, and croaked, 'Get serious!' and tried to struggle off the sofa. But he moved closer, imperceptibly, but definitely closer, the warmth of his body, the musky male scent of him immobilising her by sensation alone.

Forcing a defensive tinge of asperity to her tone, she told him, 'How could you expect me to do anything so insane? We barely know each other, we don't trust each other, and we certainly don't love each other!'

'Ah——' His face was very close to hers. She could see the tiny gold flecks that tipped the individual thick black lashes. And something in the endless transparency of those devilish green eyes held her in thrall, effortlessly trapping her by the force of his will alone as he contradicted, 'Love's an illusion. Who needs it? People use it to justify the primitive need to mate. And, for my part, I know you very well. Through Martin I know you as well as I know any other human being. I've liked what he's told me about you, and when I saw you I knew I wanted you. The urge to take you to bed astonished me by its basic and powerful primeval strength. I've already told you I have the need to settle and raise a family. That being so——' his grin disarmed her, as it was meant to, she recognised feebly as his hand curved tormentingly on the underside of one shamelessly aroused breast '—why should I waste time looking for a suitable mate, go through all that insincere courting ritual, when I have the woman I want right here—for the taking?'

Selina opened her mouth to protest she'd rather be dead, but he stopped her words with the pressure of his mouth, whispering against her breath, 'We'll grow to trust each other in time. And respect will grow from that. It's enough for me. And for you——' He freed her lips, searching her eyes with lazy penetration, recognising the tiny, not quite extinguished light of defiance in the golden depths, and murmured, 'For you there will be the satisfaction of knowing you have saved your uncle's business, home and reputation, that you have done what countless others before you have done—married for sound business and financial reasons. And for us there is always the bonus of sexual chemistry.' His hand moved to cover her breast as it thrust against the constraining wisp of lace and his voice went ragged as he asked, 'I'll prove it to you, shall I?'

CHAPTER SIX

'NO! PLEASE!' Selina didn't need him to prove it. She was fully aware of the overwhelmingly powerful physical attraction. Every time she saw him, every time he touched her it hit her between the eyes like a sledge-hammer, damaging her brain.

But his lips swallowed her breathy protest and, as he'd said earlier, it was no contest. And her last coherent thought, before hedonistic sensuality laid her brain waste, was that maybe it was the same for him. Maybe he, too, felt this overpowering, intense physical need...

Blindly, her hands slithered between the open edges of his shirt, her palms flattened against his wide, rawly male chest, her fingers splayed as they found his shoulders, curling into the burning skin as his tongue raided the sweet and helplessly willing interior of her mouth.

She was dizzy with the newness of what he was doing to her, the way he was making her feel. It was gorgeous, it was heaven, and who cared that her emotions were too basic to be controlled by a conscious effort of will? She wriggled closer, she couldn't get close enough, her mind stubbornly refusing to function until, shocking her, he broke contact, removing his hands from their intimate and blindingly sensual enjoyment of her aching breasts, removing his lips from hers and dragging her fingers from their eager exploration of the tormenting, tantalising demarcation zone at the waistband of his trousers.

'So much enthusiasm,' he said, a hint of dryness sharpening the husky tone of his voice as he captured her fluttering hands between one of his. There was a curve of smugness lying over the sensual beauty of his mouth and his eyes were narrowed, as if he knew it all as he told her, 'I didn't need to prove a thing, did I?' His strong, long-fingered hands tightened over hers. 'Admit it.'

She would do no such thing. At least, not to him. She had never felt so ashamed of herself in her life. And sullen hatred glowered at him from her long golden eyes and intensified into glittering, dagger-like shards as he simply shrugged, released her hands, said, 'Stubborn, hmm?' and levered himself to his feet before bending down to retrieve the shirt buttons she'd popped in her wanton gusto to touch every available inch of his skin.

He faced her then, turning smoothly on his heels, tossing the pearly buttons from one hand to the other, his expression unreadable. Selina looked at the carpet. The exposed expanse of utterly masculine chest made embarrassed colour crawl over her face.

How could she? How could she have hurled herself at him that way, practically ravishing him, tearing the clothes off his back in her intoxicated need to get closer? She disgusted herself. And, what was even worse, he'd implied that they'd be good together sexually and she'd gone straight ahead and proved him right, damn him!

Willing herself to calm down, to salvage some dignity, she forced her strangled breathing into a more regular pattern and was feeling marginally less distraught when his cool voice told her, 'You'll need to get moving. I imagine you intend visiting Martin but before you do that I want you to try to track Dominic. I'll be visiting the hospital myself this evening and I'd like to know where the little creep is before then.'

He was tipping her out! Something remarkably like disappointment chilled her to the bone, but she covered the unwanted aberration, snapped, 'Don't give me orders! If you want him, you find him,' and stared him in the eye. He had fastened his shirt, thank heaven, even though the fabric gaped a little where the buttons were missing, but the thought of how they came to be adrift made her feel decidedly uncomfortable again so she got to her feet and said as haughtily as she could, 'My coat, please. I believe you hurled it somewhere.'

She couldn't get out of here fast enough now. She supposed he would be driving her back to the flat so that she could pick up her car and she would have to endure his pernicious company for a little while longer. And her soft mouth was set in a grim line as he bent to retrieve the leather jacket from the floor and went grimmer still when he tossed it to her, telling her, 'You find him. I've got more important things to do. You'll have a better idea where to look, which of his current lady friends is likely to have taken him in.'

Tossing her head in fury at his dictatorial manner, she bit back her refusal to do anything of the kind, remembering now what he had said. At the time, her mind had been disengaged. He had been—well, distracting her. Now she accused, 'You said something about Dominic milking the funds. What the hell were you getting at? And I'll tell you now, I won't believe a word of your lies.'

'No?' A coolly sardonic eyebrow lifted fractionally. 'You've only got to look at the books. I can prove it to you. I have enough evidence to prosecute on the bank's behalf.' He walked over the room to pick up the phone, punching numbers with an impatient finger.

Shocked into silence by his icy confidence, Selina's eyes bored into his broad back as he instructed, 'I want a car here in ten minutes,' snapping out his address before turning back to her, his face cold. But no colder than the dread that clutched at her heart as he said, almost indifferently, 'I can't spare the time to run you back myself, and I meant what I said about finding Dominic. When you run him to ground warn him that if he's thinking of leaving the country with a chunk of the bank's funds then he'd better think again. Wherever he goes, I'll find him. And the more trouble he causes me, the harder it will go for him.'

'You mean it, don't you?' Selina whispered, shaken, her face very pale as she searched his narrowed eyes for the truth. And he nodded, slowly, something like compassion softening his voice as he explained,

'Believe it, sweetheart. He's been helping himself for years, but latterly, since Martin took a back seat because of his health, he's become greedy.'

He paced to the window, looking out, shooting an impatient glance at his watch, and Selina thought, He can't wait to get rid of me, but wondering why it should hurt was stupidly unproductive so she asked tightly, 'How do you know all this?'

'By going through the books, how else?' He spread his hands, his eyes scornful, and then explained, as if to an idiot, 'When Martin first approached me for funding, the books were scrutinised by our own accountants. There were minor discrepancies—fifty here, a hundred there—but nothing that couldn't be put down to sloppy accountancy. And, believe me, Dominic's sloppy.' He shot another humiliating glance at his watch.

'But, given the bank's funding, King's Ransom wasn't making the profit it should have been. So, having a personal interest, you might say, I took a private look at the books. Over the last six months the missing sums of money amounted to thousands. As I said, given a free rein, he got greedy, and wasn't clever enough to hide what he was doing. So far, I've kept it in the family, as it were. You know what you have to do to keep it from going public.'

Marry him. He really meant it. Selina went cold all over, her eyes drifting shut, and when she opened them again he was standing over her, green flames of devilment back in his eyes as he lifted her chin with the tip of his forefinger.

'It won't be so bad, I promise.' He had brought the devastating power of that sexy voice back into play and it made her knees go weak, so weak that she almost sagged against him, but stiffened her backbone by an immense effort of will as he continued, tauntingly, 'We'll be good together, I promise you. And I won't rush you; I'm not entirely inconsiderate. A spring wedding will suit me fine—some time towards the end of March, say. It will give you time to get used to the idea. I'll tell Martin when I see him this evening.' He moved away and the next thing she knew he was pushing her bag into her nerveless hands. 'Your taxi's here; see you later.'

Not if she saw him first. That was the thought that fumed through Selina's mind all the way back to the flat. She banged the door behind her and stamped through the empty rooms. Where the hell was Dominic? The empty rooms mocked her and she sagged against the kitchen wall.

And in that bleak moment of stillness, of silence, she knew Adam had been speaking the truth.

Her cousin had always been weak. As a child he would take things that weren't his if he thought no one was looking. Handling the company's money must have been a temptation he couldn't resist. His salary was good and his parents defrayed most of his everyday living expenses, but he'd wanted more. And more. His penchant for beautiful, expensive female friends was well-known. To be seen with such exotic creatures was a boost to his ego. He didn't seem to mind that they all had cash registers where other people had hearts.

Quite suddenly, she hated Dominic with a venom she hadn't known herself to possess. He and his greed and vanity had put her where she was now. And that was firmly in Adam Tudor's power. A most unenviable place to be. Marry him or he'd prosecute, make sure Dominic faced the full consequences of his avarice.

If it weren't for Martin's precarious state of health she might be inclined to let the law take its course. It would teach him the lesson that he couldn't steal and cheat and lie with impunity—a lesson his doting mother had signally failed to drum into his precious, swollen head!

But her affection for her uncle wouldn't let her do anything of the kind. The shock when his son and heir was banged behind bars would probably kill him. And there was worse, oh, wasn't there just!

Marry Adam, or not only would he put his half-brother in gaol, he would make sure the bank foreclosed, taking just about everything Martin had worked so hard for over the years.

She ground her teeth. She couldn't imagine why her normally astute uncle had gone to his loathsome son for funding in the first place; there were other merchant banks, for pity's sake! And from what she now knew they had kept in touch through the years, so surely Martin must have picked up at least a hint of the resentment that had driven his illegitimate son so far down the road to revenge?

And then she thought of something truly, truly awful. That monster had told her he would visit Martin again, some time this evening—to tell him about their forthcoming marriage!

How he would gloat as he impressed the fact that the elderly man's devoted adopted daughter was being used in a sick game of revenge and coercion. Knowing there was nothing he could do to safeguard his adopted daughter's happiness, wrest her out of his odious son's clutches, would distress him utterly. To let her off the hook he would have to sacrifice Dominic and everything he had ever worked for. He would be in an impossible situation.

She had to get to him first!

Galvanised into action at last, she locked up and ran down to her car. Adam had instructed her to try to find her cousin—well, he could go boil his head, and so could Dominic! She had to see Martin and, somehow or other, soften the blow. Quite how she had no idea. But she'd think of something.

'Well? Did you find him?' Vanessa asked and Selina shook her head. The strain was beginning to show; the older woman's habitual poise was coming adrift.

'He wasn't at the flat, and from the look of the place he hasn't been near except to activate the answering machine.' She didn't say that she hadn't bothered to look further, that she'd spent the morning being made love to by the despised and hated Adam Tudor, that she'd returned to the Hall when he'd turned her out of his house to figure out what to do, or that when she'd finally come up with a workable plan she'd had a quick shower and taken the time and care to dress the part.

Vanessa swore, a coarse oath that made Selina's eyebrows shoot up to her hairline. Her aunt had been under a dreadful strain lately, she thought as she watched the other woman drag a coat out of the cupboard in the side-room she'd been using to stay near her husband. Did she know what trouble her precious son was in? Selina wondered, dragging her lower lip between her teeth. Had she realised he'd been fiddling the books and had simply stood idly by, unable to deny her adored offspring anything, not even stolen money?

Impossible. And her certainty of her aunt's complete honesty was reinforced when Vanessa grabbed her handbag and held out her hand, her voice quick and sharp as she commanded, 'Give me your car keys. I'm going back to the house. I know where he keeps his address book and I'll phone around until I find where he is.' She clicked her fingers impatiently as Selina rooted in her bag for the keys, moving her weight from one foot to the other. 'The poor boy's ill, too sick to make contact. He's got to be. Nothing else would explain his apparent disappearance, the way he hasn't once contacted me to find out how his father is.' She took the keys held out to her and practically hurled herself from the room, and Selina shook her head and sighed.

Right now Dominic would be holed up somewhere, frightened to put his nose round the door in case Adam Tudor jumped on him and hauled him off to face charges of embezzlement or fraud or whatever. His refusal to hang around and face his half-brother, when Selina had all but begged him to, now made a whole lot of sense.

His poor mother would have the shock of her life when she discovered the truth.

But at the moment Dominic was the very least of her worries. She removed her scarlet wool coat and hooked it over her arm, reflecting that the way her fingers trembled was no bad thing, not really. This edgy, half-scared, half-exhilarated sensation, this feeling that she was about to launch herself off the edge of a towering cliff, would actually help her in the part she had elected to play.

Her poor duped uncle would put her jitters down to excitement and nerves. But better duped than dead. The shock of learning that his beloved niece was being used in a sick game of blackmail could, in his present state of health, finish him off. She wasn't going to stand by and see that happen.

She dragged in a deep breath. Now for it. But first she made time to take a reassuring look in the mirror on top of the tiny dressing-chest. A heavier hand than usual with the make-up had successfully hidden the pallor and strain. The shimmer of gold shadow over her eyes made them look sparkling, like fine topaz, the mascaraed thick lashes adding the right touch of hazed dreaminess, the tawny lipstick giving her mouth a glossy sheen that emphasised its sultry, pouting curves, toning exactly with the fine wool dress that fitted her so perfectly that it was almost sinful.

Pushing her unsteady hands through her hair, re-inforcing the wild abandon of the tawny, gold-streaked riot, she walked out of the room on teetering scarlet heels, and across the quiet corridor to Martin's room.

'Oh—you look so much better!' Selina cried delightedly as she dropped her coat over the back of a chair and rushed to the bedside to plant an affectionate kiss on his cheek.

It was such a relief! That awful greyness had left his face, so had the look of anxiety. He looked quite back to normal, and that was a bonus she hadn't dared to hope for, and he grinned at her.

'I'm fighting fit, can't remember feeling better.' His eyes twinkled at her. 'Pull up a chair and tell me who's the lucky man. You didn't make yourself look so stunningly gorgeous just to visit me!'

She did as she was told, dragging an armchair close to the side of the bed so that she could hold his hand, veiling her eyes. So her strategy was working, and the slight, unaccountable blush she felt creep across her skin could only add a veneer of veracity to the lies she was going to have to tell him.

'Well, I don't know——' She broke off, suddenly and uncharacteristically hesitant, found her teeth gnawing at her lower lip and stopped herself before she unwittingly transferred all that carefully applied lipstick to her teeth and ended up looking less than perfect and rather silly by the time Adam Tudor arrived. 'I don't know how you're going to take this,' she ploughed stoically on, burning her boats, 'but since you were taken ill I've seen a lot of your son—Adam, that is.' She flicked him a doubtful glance from beneath thickly fringing lashes— oh, God, this was just dreadful!—met the heightened intenseness of his eyes and looked quickly away again, her fingers twisting together in her lap.

If she could convince him that she had fallen head over heels in love with the brute, then, for her sake, he would accept the talk of marriage as he would never, with any honour or tranquillity, accept a state of coercion. For his own peace of mind she had to convince him. So she said, sounding breathless, 'I don't know quite how it happened, but we fell in love. Crazy, isn't it?' She attempted a laugh which didn't come off. 'He's asked me to marry him.'

'And you've accepted.' Spoken quietly, it wasn't really a question, but he didn't sound shocked.

She risked another glance and felt her breath catch in her throat. He was smiling. He actually looked pleased! She stared, her eyes going wide. All her preconceptions were being turned upside-down. She didn't know where she was any more.

And now wasn't the time to try to figure anything out and she nodded mutely, unable to speak, and heard him say, 'Adam's existence has been a well-kept secret—out of deference to your aunt, you understand—and I'm glad you two have met at last. He's a fine human being and I knew, if you ever did meet, you'd get along famously.' He chuckled drily. 'Quite how famously I hadn't bargained for.'

'You don't mind?' she asked breathlessly, feeling poleaxed, and he patted her hand, his voice warm as he assured her,

'I'm delighted,' then, his tone more sober, 'Have you broken the news to your aunt yet?' receiving a shake of her tawny head. 'I think you'd better leave that to me. She's, well, understandably touchy where Adam's concerned. And you can ask Adam to tell you about his mother. He's the best person to do that.'

Ha! Selina snorted inside her head. She could just see the Think-I-Am-God Adam Tudor relishing a conversation about such a sleazy set-up. She could just see him confiding how his promiscuous parent had set out to ensnare a much younger man, a man hardly out of his teens if her arithmetic was correct, trying to trap him into marriage with the oldest trick in the book—how she'd fastened herself to what she saw as a bottomless bank balance for the rest of her life.

Outwardly, though, she smiled sweetly, lowering her lids to hide the gleam of triumph in her long amber eyes. She had successfully spiked Adam's evil guns. By committing herself, lying about a whirlwind romance, love that had blossomed at first sight, she had thwarted his rotten need for revenge and power. He couldn't walk in here and gloat about the way he was blackmailing her into a loveless marriage, throwing the older man into a vortex of panic and frustration.

She had gambled on Martin's putting her happiness before all else, and quite why he had called Adam a 'fine human being' she couldn't imagine, and didn't have time to ask and find out because she could hear the wretch in the corridor outside, talking to one of the nursing staff, and she was going to need all her concentration to carry the next phase off convincingly——

Which she managed with a thoroughness that surprised her when, her smile as sweet as treacle and just as sickly on her tongue, she burbled the moment he walked through the door, 'Darling—I thought you were never coming! And I'm sorry, I know we planned to break the news together but I was so ecstatic about everything I simply couldn't wait.' She forced herself to her feet and flew to his side, standing on tiptoe to kiss him lingeringly on lips she found too willing for comfort, then, tucking her arm through his, her fingers clutching the expensive dark grey fabric of his beautifully tailored overcoat, she batted her lashes and husked, 'I've confessed everything—how we took one look at each other and fell in love.'

Had she gone too far over the top? she wondered, panic beating a wriggly path through her veins as Adam's glittering eyes searched hers. But apparently not, she sighed with relief as he stroked her hand and gave it back to her while he walked over to his father's bedside and put an affectionate hand on the older man's pyjama-clad shoulder, telling him, with a sincerity in his voice that surely couldn't be real, 'I'm glad to see you looking so much better. I rang your consultant earlier this afternoon and got a good progress report—so mind you keep it up!' And then he turned, shafting a smile that was sheer hungry tiger in Selina's direction as he continued talking to Martin. 'So you've heard all about our wedding plans? We fixed a tentative date for the end of March, so you should be properly back on your feet by then and able to enjoy the celebrations. And it will give Selina enough time to find a wedding gown that will do full justice to her beauty.'

Lying devil! Selina's toes curled, his smile, his voice, the way his eyes were lazily and appreciatively devouring her body all contributing to her agitation. He had entered the web of deceit she had woven with all the aplomb of a seasoned chiseller, playing his part as if he'd written the scene himself. She had expected him to fumble his lines, expected some signs of annoyance at the way she'd turned the tables on him, denying him the opportunity to gloat over the sick man's helpless discomfiture. As far as revenge went, he was being short-changed.

So she gave him back a smile that reflected her inner satisfaction in having bested him for once, a smile she was hard pressed to hang on to as he stalked the few paces to her side and gathered her in his arms.

Martin was saying something about arrangements, about how pleased he was for them both. But for once she wasn't taking a blind bit of notice of her uncle because the way Adam's one hand was fondling the curvy swell of her buttocks, the other resting perilously near the underside of her breasts, was doing disastrous things to her blood-pressure.

The devil was playing to the gallery—wasn't he just?—and there wasn't a thing she could do about it without arousing Martin's suspicions. But silent endurance had never been her style and, a silly smile pinned to her face, she was wondering if Martin would notice if she drove the spike of her heel down hard on Adam's instep when that husky, ravishingly sexy voice said, 'Yes, of course Selina will be married from the Hall, but we've decided she'll move in with me until a couple of days before the wedding. Now we've found each other, we can't bear to be apart for more than a few moments at a time. Isn't that right, my darling?'

What the hell could she say to that? Out of sight, Adam's hand was lovingly stroking her bottom, the wicked, slow smile on his sensuous lips leaving her in no doubt that he knew exactly what he was doing to her. And Martin was grinning, lifting his shoulders in a wry shrug, saying, 'I understand. Why not? I hear it's the modern equivalent of an engagement. Besides——' he shook his head in mock despair '—I know both of you well enough to expect you to do exactly as you please.'

For the first time in her life Selina wanted to hit her beloved uncle. Why couldn't he have come over all old-fashioned for once, been just a bit outraged? And she couldn't scream at Adam to take his filthy hands off her and leave him in no doubt that she had no intention of shacking up with him before the wedding—probably not after it, either. That would undo all the good work she'd put in here.

So she said nothing, nothing at all as Adam helped her into her coat, letting his clever, insinuating hands glide over her when he'd finished settling it on her shoulders. She just hoped Martin would construe her angry colour as maidenly modesty. And she bit her tongue, biding her time until she could tell Adam Casanova Tudor exactly what he could do with his outrageous try-ons!

CHAPTER SEVEN

'WE'LL call at the Hall and pick up your things on the way.'

Adam had the car door open for her and Selina came to a breathless standstill. As they'd left the hospital she had been forced to run to keep up with his long loping pace, which, wearing the highest heels she owned, hadn't been fun and hadn't given her the opportunity to castigate him for telling Martin they'd be living together until the wedding, either.

'You can drop me off,' she told him, trying to catch her breath. Vanessa had borrowed her car so he might as well. It would save her having to phone for a taxi. 'I've no intention of moving in with you. And if telling Martin we'd decided to do that was your idea of a joke it didn't amuse me.'

It was dusk now, the winter day drawing to a close, and the lights of the hospital car park made his face look menacing. He said, 'It was no joke.'

A shudder ran through her as he slammed the door and strode round the front of the car but she told herself staunchly that he couldn't make her move in with him, at least not until after the wedding he was maniacally intent on forcing her into.

If there was to be a wedding. A lot could happen in two months, and if she appeared to go along with the idea, allowed him to think he'd got her under his thumb, then he'd get a sense of security, however false, and she'd get a breathing space. And she needed that space. Time to plot how to wriggle out of his clutches and frustrate his need for revenge. She didn't quite know how she'd manage it, but she'd think of something.

But pretending to agree to a wedding was one thing, sharing his roof in the interim was something else. So, as he slid in beside her and started the engine, she said stubbornly, 'You can't make me move in with you.'

'True.' He didn't bother to look at her, just concentrated on backing the Mercedes out of the parking space. And only when they were heading out of town towards Lower Otterley, only when she was congratulating herself on having won that round without even getting out of breath, did he bother to deliver the knock-out blow, 'I can't make you move in, but won't Martin think it strange if you're still at the Hall? After the convincing show you put on back there, the pretty blushes and dimpling smiles when I told him we'd be living together until the wedding, he'll begin to think something's gone wrong if we don't.'

'Pretty blushes and dimpling smiles'! Didn't he recognise a flush of anger, a snarl of rage, when he saw one? He was making her sound like a wimp! She'd show him she wasn't and, her face burning with fury, she was trying to work her way out of the corner he'd backed her into when he said softly, huskily, 'I can't figure out why you've suddenly decided that marrying me is your idea of heaven, with bells on, but I'm not about to knock it. I loved the way you threw yourself at me. I couldn't keep my hands off you. Can you blame me for jumping the gun when it came to our living arrangements? I foresee an interesting, if practically sleepless future for us—so don't go all coy on me now, sweetheart!'

'Coy?' she shrieked back at him, then clamped her mouth shut. He was laughing at her, damn him. He had

hoist her with her own petard! And he needn't pretend
he didn't know why she had staged that charade. He
must know she'd only done it to stop him gloating about
his successful blackmail attempts to Martin.

'Yes, I admit it's about the last adjective I'd choose
to describe you, sweetheart,' he murmured soothingly,
the trace of laughter in his voice infuriating her. 'So we'll
forget all about your little attack of maidenly modesty,
shall we? It never happened.'

'Pompous, scheming, unscrupulous chiseller!' she
muttered into her coat collar, hunching her shoulders.
She squeezed her eyes shut, thinking hard.

As he'd said, it would be difficult to explain to Martin
why she was still at the Hall and not shacking up with
his hateful first-born, especially as the lying hound had
said they'd already decided they couldn't bear to be apart
for a single moment. And she hadn't denied it, because
by then it had been too late. She'd been acting and talking
as if she were besotted, couldn't wait to change her name
to Tudor, had fallen in love with him as if that emotion
were in danger of becoming obsolete!

'Don't take all night about it, you can always collect
more of your stuff later,' Adam instructed, and Selina
reluctantly opened her eyes, knowing she had no other
option at the moment, not if Martin was to be kept in
blissful ignorance of the true state of affairs.

He drew up on the gravelled forecourt, the Mercedes's
headlights illuminating her Volvo parked in front of the
door, and she said thinly, all the stuffing suddenly
knocked out of her, 'What about my car?' her mind not
so much occupied with that but with Vanessa's reaction
to her news that she was moving in with the hated and
feared Adam Tudor, the grisly skeleton in the family
closet.

'Leave it. We can pick it up some other time. Right now I'm in a tearing hurry to get back to my place. I'm hungry. And even if you're not we both know how easily I can stimulate your appetite.'

And what was that supposed to mean? Better not ask, she decided huffily, scrambling out of the car, telling him when he silently appeared at her side as she stepped into the hall, 'There's no need for you to come in. Wait in the car.'

But he walked right in beside her, the grip of his hand on her elbow a warning, his voice low and smoky as he bent his dark head towards hers.

'You might change your mind and lock me out, and I wouldn't like you to have to suffer the consequences of doing anything that misguided. And don't forget I hold the deeds here; the Hall is as good as mine.'

He closed the huge oak door behind them on that softly spoken warning, gave her backside an intimate pat and walked towards the woodburner.

'I'll wait here. If you're not down in five minutes I'll come and get you. Your eagerness at Martin's bedside has whetted my appetite.'

Hateful wretch! He had to know it had been an act. He was winding her up with a vengeance, and once they were out of here, at his home, she would have it out with him once and for all.

She moved quickly but quietly. There was no sign of Vanessa, or Meg, and she wanted to keep it that way. Cowardice was a new and unwelcome sensation but she just knew what her aunt's reaction to the news that she was moving in with Adam would be. She didn't think she could stand one more trauma just yet. She'd already lived through enough to last her a lifetime.

Hurriedly, she tossed a few overnight things into a bag, plus a change of clothing for the morning and, practically holding her breath, made the long journey back through the house.

Adam was where she had left him, his back to the stove, his eyes alight with what she interpreted as malicious triumph as he took the soft fabric travel bag from her and steered her out through the door.

It was only as she was fastening her seatbelt with shaky fingers that she noticed the Volvo was missing and her heart skipped a beat. Vanessa. She would have had to walk right past her husband's despised bastard and... It didn't bear thinking about, but she had to know.

She moistened her dry lips with a nervous flick of her tongue, her words sounding strangled above the quiet purr of the engine as she asked, 'Did you see my aunt leave?'

'Indeed I did.' His voice almost throbbed with self-satisfaction. 'We had an interesting conversation. Short, but interesting.'

He seemed disinclined to enlighten her further, apparently concentrating totally on the road. And if he had taken his thwarted revenge out on Vanessa, gloating about blackmail and all that stuff, she would kill him!

Vanessa would relay the whole conversation to Martin and the sharp-clawed cat would be well and truly out of the bag!

'So what was so interesting?' she enquired tightly, all ready to do him some violent physical damage if he confirmed her suspicions. But he took the breath out of her lungs when he told her,

'She told me where I could find dear Dominic.'

'What?' She couldn't believe it. Her head snapped round, registered the small smile that softened his hard profile, and knew he was telling the truth.

'Helpful of her, wasn't it?' The smooth tone sharpened. 'Did you know?'

She shook her head. Her life was taking on an Alice in Wonderland quality: she no longer knew what was real, what was illusion. And her tongue felt thick in her mouth as she answered, 'No. How could I have done? Vanessa didn't know either. She borrowed my car to go back home. She knew where he kept his address book and was going to phone around.'

Her mumbled reply seemed to have satisfied him, because he put a hand on her leg, just above her knee, squeezing just once and lingeringly before replacing it back on the wheel, and his voice was low and sexy as he imparted, 'Then she was obviously successful. He's holed up somewhere in Battersea with a professional model by the name of Roxy l'Amour,' and, at Selina's strangled croak, he added, 'Amazing, isn't it? Her real name's probably Doris Peabody.'

Selina ground her teeth together. She wasn't interested in Dominic's latest's wretched name! She was interested in the methods he'd used to obtain that information. Vanessa wouldn't willingly have told him the time of day.

'So what did you do?' she asked drily. 'Twist her arm?' And why hadn't Vanessa attempted to throw him out? Or did she know how deeply in debt the company was to the creature?

'Not my style, sweetheart.' The rough velvet voice sent shivers right down her spine and, annoyed that he could still have that effect on her, she sniped, reminding herself of how hateful he was,

'No, you prefer blackmail, don't you? How silly of me to forget.'

'Watch your tongue, sweetheart.' But he didn't sound annoyed, more amused than anything, as if he found the whole sorry mess a joke, just a pleasant diversion, his voice laced with lazy, curling contempt as he amplified, 'Put it this way—she told me what I wanted to know when I made her see it was impossible to refuse.'

And what that meant was anyone's guess, Selina muttered inside her head. Then closed her eyes. All at once she was unbelievably tired, the strain of the last days getting through to her. She couldn't stand any more of this in-fighting; it was sapping her energy, muddling her mind. And she was still feeling weakly disorientated, tearful, too, when they arrived at his mews cottage. She would need all her energy, all her wits, if she was to keep him at arm's length. And just when she needed all that strength and determination the most it seemed to have deserted her.

'You've had about as much as you can take, haven't you, sweetheart?'

So the outside security light must have illuminated the distress she'd been trying to hide beneath a mask of indifference. And the soft timbre of his voice, the concern, almost made her believe he cared. But she squashed that notion for the foolishness it was and the fight was back behind her voice, the stiffening back in her spine, as she rejected the supporting arm he slid around her waist and stalked through to the room she had been in earlier.

'Let's get one thing clear,' she announced, swinging on her spiky heels to face him. 'You may have made it impossible for me to stay on at the Hall, but I'm not staying here. I've got a couple of things I want to say to you and then you can run me over to Martin's town flat, or I'll phone for a taxi. I don't mind which.'

'My town flat,' he reminded her, his eyes going hard. 'Have you forgotten that Martin is no longer the legal owner?'

'A hotel, then!' she flashed, her eyes, the set of her chin showing just how much she hated him. 'Or are you going to use blackmail again to keep me here?'

The devilish gleam in his wicked green eyes showed her how utterly stupid she'd been. She had handed him the means on a plate. If she hadn't mouthed off he might not have thought of that!

She moaned with self-contempt, misery dragging her mouth down, making her close her eyes to block out a world that had suddenly grown twisted and devious, a world where she no longer seemed able to control her destiny.

And then the moan deepened, catching at the back of her throat as his warm lips lightly covered hers, and inevitably, shamingly, she wasn't fighting, telling him to push off, wasn't even considering such a sensible course of action. The alien world she had found herself in suddenly receded, leaving nothing but sheer mind-blowing sensation, the warm, breathtakingly teasing touch of light kisses as his lips tasted hers.

The kiss was so breathtaking that her bones turned to heavy liquid, incapable of supporting her, making the way her arms moved with slow, inexorable grace to twine around his neck a matter of inescapable necessity. And then his arms moved to hold her, tightening, drawing her fluid body close to the masculine hardness of his, his tongue outlining her parted lips, teasing the corners of her mouth until she opened wider, almost sobbing in

her need to have him taste her, delve within the moist,
honey-sweet depths.

And then he did, and her world shattered into brilliant
shards of sheer sensuality, shards that lanced with sharply
sweet explosions through every vein, every nerve-ending.
She felt giddy, melting, an intense yet unnamed hunger
making her press her body closer to his, grinding her
hips against the aroused hardness of his, her tongue
fighting a duel of desire with his. And then she went
into shock as he growled a terse expletive, dragging her
clinging arms from their stranglehold around his neck
and thrust her away, holding her at arm's length.

Dazed golden eyes searched the glittering, narrowed
brilliance of his, found a glimmer of contempt that
turned her blood to ice, then dropped with incompre-
hension to the taut line of the mouth that had so recently been moving with expert sensuality against her
own.

Dragging her hands from his punitive grasp, she
stepped backward, trying to pull herself together. She
didn't understand. Her body was a minefield of un-
explained needs, inexplicable rejection, and she heard
him say, as if nothing at all had happened, 'I'll show
you to the room you can use. You might have to share
my roof but there's no need for you to share my bed.'
He picked up her overnight bag and walked coolly to
the door, gesturing her to follow. 'Perhaps you'd like to
freshen up while I fix supper.'

Crazy. Everything was crazy, nothing was as it seemed.
Selina followed bewilderedly, hardly heard a word of
what he said as he opened the door to what was obviously a guest room, explaining about *en suite* fa-
cilities, and stood staring blankly into space as he left.

Her body was still plagued by the raging needs he had so easily awakened and she ground her teeth, trying to subdue them. One moment he had been kissing her as if he couldn't get enough of her, the next he had thrust her away, telling her insultingly that she needn't expect to share his bed, looking at her as if she were beneath contempt. Why?

She shook her head in hopeless confusion and, more to take her mind off her uncomfortable state of sexual arousal than out of any real interest, began to pace the room.

It might have been a room in a first-class hotel, perfect yet impersonal, the furniture top-of-the-range contemporary, the curtains and carpet understated luxury, obviously fabulously expensive. The adjoining bathroom was a revelation of ceiling-to-floor smoked-glass mirrors, deep burgundy porcelain fitments, white marble floor and lush green ferns in white china bowls.

With an unwilling sigh of appreciation, she turned back to the bedroom, kicked off the high-heeled scarlet shoes, hung her coat in the wall-length wardrobe and unzipped her dress. Her packing had been hurried, done without thought. She pulled a short, beautifully fitting straight black skirt from the bag, a collarless oyster silk blouse and a nightdress that was Janet Reger at her most sybaritic.

As Martin had correctly deduced, she had dressed to look gorgeous, determined that her appearance would add veracity to her unlikely statement that she and Adam had fallen deeply, passionately in love. She couldn't bear to face him again wearing the sexy, tawny dress. But the black skirt and almost transparent silk blouse would hardly look less of a sexual invitation.

Selina groaned, gave up trying to think and padded through to the bathroom to shower. And it was while the hot needles of water were stinging her body that her brain finally cleared. She knew what was happening and, despite the heat of the water, her body went cold.

Her mane of hair plastered to her skull, hanging in wet wrinkles down her back, she stepped out and smothered herself in one of the huge, burgundy-coloured bath-sheets.

His plan for revenge was deeper and dirtier than she had suspected, she thought, a stab of pain deep inside her making her flinch. One of his reasons for forcing her into marriage had been the undoubted and potent sexual attraction between them—unwilling yet inescapable on her part.

She now knew that simply wasn't true.

Redoubling her efforts to towel most of the moisture out of her hair, she clamped her teeth together and faced the unpalatable facts. His side of the chemical sexual equation simply didn't exist. Twice now he had thrust her away from him at the moment when her control had been non-existent. Twice.

He was experienced enough—who could doubt it?—to know that she found his physical attractions overpowering, overwhelming enough to block out her distrust and dislike of his character. Yet she left him cold. He could steel himself to demonstrate how effortlessly he could bring her to the point of complete, willing and wanton capitulation and, having reached that point, couldn't wait to push her away. And downstairs, less than an hour ago, he hadn't been able to hide his contempt for her.

All along the line he had pretended to want her physically, obviously taking a malicious pleasure in arousing her, planning a truly Machiavellian revenge. He would force her to marry him—and burn, and after the consuming flames watch her slowly shrivel in the sterile relationship of an empty marriage. Empty of respect, of shared needs, of the children he had lied about wanting.

He was cold, calculating and cruel. And, strangely, accepting that undeniable fact made her want to cry.

Putting it down to her complete loss of what she had once held so dear—her self-respect—she dropped the towel in a crumpled damp heap on the floor, not caring. Let him tidy up after her if it bothered him. She hadn't asked to come here. Then she stiffened, holding her breath as she heard the rap of his knuckles on her bedroom door.

He wouldn't wait forever, her agitated mind informed her. He'd walk right in and find her naked and think she was begging for his wretched body! Beginning to panic now, she dragged the towelling robe hanging on the back of the door with a sob of relief and thrust her arms into the overlong sleeves, snatching the edges together and tying the belt so tightly around her waist that she felt in danger of being cut in two.

She reached the door just as the porcelain knob was beginning to turn and dragged it open, turning away immediately because she wasn't yet strong enough to meet his eyes—not with her recent discovery of how brutally scheming he really was so fresh in her mind.

Not that she had really wanted him to make love to her, she reminded herself tartly. Her own body was the traitor here.

'Supper's ready. I hope you like pasta; I'm not much good with anything else.'

The husky, disgracefully sexy tone of his voice reached out to her, enfolding her, and, hate herself as she did for instinctively responding to it, she hated him even more. Her back still to him, she hunched her shoulders dismissively, her own voice low and sullen as she told him, 'I don't want anything. I'm going to bed. Goodnight.'

'You'll eat even if I have to force it down your throat,' he threatened on a drag of impatience. And then, walking to stand directly in front of her, his tone more reasonable, he said, 'Like me, you've probably been too busy to think of food all day.' And his unreadable eyes swept her mutinous features, a smile as insincere as any she had seen curving the cruel lines of his beautiful mouth. 'Why turn a simple supper for two into a war?'

Why indeed? She dragged her unwilling gaze from his and averted her head. She had to be strong, fight him on his own terms. Take the battle to him, if necessary. And she was strong; of course she was. Already she was coming to terms with the unpalatable revelations this evening had brought and soon she would understand how to counter them, perhaps make them work for her. And when she did she would be stronger than ever!

With a proud tilt of her head she turned and looked him coldly in the eye, her voice displaying no trace of emotion as she accepted, 'If you'll excuse my state of untidy undress at the table...'

And he grinned, almost disarming her all over again.

'Untidy you may be——' His wicked eyes roved over the untamed tawny mane of her hair, dried into wild, wrinkling curls because she hadn't bothered to try to style it. 'Undressed, you ain't—I've never found floor-to-earlobe towelling much of a turn-on. You'll be quite safe.'

And so she would be, she vowed, following him down the stairs, carefully lifting the hem of the smothering over-large robe to avoid tripping. When she had believed his sexual advances to be genuine, his needs as explosive as her own, the hitherto unsuspected sensuality which lurked inside her had made it impossible for her to resist him. But now she knew he felt nothing, had been using that fatal attraction for his own diabolical ends, she could counter it. The self-respect that was such an intrinsic part of her nature would not allow her to do less.

A low table between two armchairs which flanked the fire bore evidence of his industry—red wine and glasses, covered dishes, cutlery and plates. He lifted the cover of one of the dishes and her nostrils twitched at the savoury aroma, her stomach reminding her that she was very hungry indeed, her normal healthy appetite having been ignored in the topsy-turvy happenings of the day.

The sauce he had prepared for the pasta was delicious, succulent chunks of vegetables—mushrooms, celery, tiny onions—all in a rich tomato binding with just the right amount of oregano and garlic for her palate. The wine was good, too, she thought, clearing her plate and unashamedly accepting a second helping of food, another glass of wine.

Adam had changed out of his formal suit and was now wearing black cords that fitted the narrow span of his hips and the muscled length of his legs far too perfectly for her peace of mind. And the black V-necked sweater he had chosen made the most of his wide, rangy shoulders and made her stomach flip whenever she looked at him.

So she didn't look; she kept her eyes on her plate and made only terse responses to his conversational gambits, making her mind concentrate on how she was going to handle the hateful situation she was so completely tangled up in. And when she had it sorted out to her satisfaction she finished the last scrap of food, put down her fork and told him, 'I'll marry you if I have to, for Martin's sake. But I'll do my utmost to find a way out of it.' She did look at him then, her eyes coldly defiant, sliding away when she saw the way his mouth tightened, the way one brow rose as he responded brutally,

'You won't find a way, so don't waste your time looking.'

There was something so utterly final about that statement. Selina laced her fingers together, feeling cold in spite of the fire, the soft central heating, the smothering folds of her borrowed robe. It underlined what she had known all along. There was no way out—except for the one she couldn't take.

She'd been acting like a fool, she acknowledged, an unconscious moue of self-derision pulling at the corners of her mouth. She told herself she'd beat him at his own game, somehow, not having the least idea of how she'd do it. Fooling herself, and, let's face it, enjoying the fact that he appeared to fancy her rotten. Yes, enjoying it, damn it, despite all her hot air and bluster! Lusting after the swine! And all the time he hadn't wanted her at all. It had all been a grotesque twist along the tortuous route of his planned revenge.

Her mouth hardened. It was time they both stopped playing games. If she had to marry him, and it appeared there was no 'if' about it, then everything had to be out in the open, nothing hidden.

She stuffed her hands into the capacious pockets of her robe and leaned back in the chair, doing her best to appear relaxed and in control. And her voice was clipped as she asked him, 'Have you really thought this thing through? They say revenge is sweet, but a couple of years on you might find it turning sour on you. It won't be much fun being tied to a woman you don't want, a woman who doesn't even like you——'

'Who said I don't want you?' he cut her short, that sexy, smoky purr back in his voice. And before she could counter that he'd proved, twice, that his wanting was an act, manufactured to gratify his dark need for revenge and that she wouldn't fall for that ploy again, he went on, 'And what has revenge got to do with anything?'

As if he didn't know! Her eyes locked with his, registered the glint of enquiry in the startling green depths, and dropped again as an unwilling twist of compassion unfurled within her.

He must have had a terrible childhood, feeling that his father had rejected him, learning, as he grew up, what a scheming tramp his mother really was. And he'd obviously had more contact with his father than Vanessa realised—letters and meetings. And, just as obviously, Martin had talked about his home, his family, had allowed his affection for his orphaned niece to come through very clearly.

Adam must have felt very insecure, doubted his worth, when he'd learned that Martin's niece had been taken in, been given love and support and every material comfort while he, Martin's own flesh and blood, had been rejected, hidden away as if he were something second-rate and shameful.

Despite what she knew of the man that child had become, pity flooded Selina's tender heart and her eyes were misty as she told him, 'Rejection's hard to bear. You must have grown up hating your father, especially when he gave me a home, every advantage, and wouldn't allow you over the doorstep.' Her eyes met his, unashamed tears making them glitter. 'But revenge isn't the answer. Taking all Martin's ever worked for away from him, locking me in a loveless marriage isn't going to make you feel better, not in the long run.'

'You certainly have an imagination—and make good use of it.' Amazingly, he laughed, getting to his feet and stalking over to a side-table which held a variety of carved crystal decanters. 'Unfortunately, you've come up with a few wrong numbers. Brandy?' The neck of a decanter clinked against two glasses and Selina frowned, coming back quickly,

'Have I really? Then tell me what's behind your sordid blackmail tactics.'

'Not revenge, you can be sure of that.' He put one of the glasses on the table in front of her and stood with his back to the fire, cradling his own in both hands. 'Let's go along with your amazing scenario, shall we? Take it to its logical conclusion.' His fantastically sexy mouth curved in an ironic smile, his eyes holding her frankly and defiantly disbelieving gaze. 'I want revenge for childhood wrongs. I get the opportunity to ruin my father and the half-brother I resent so jealously. Right?' A dark eyebrow drifted upwards, inviting a comment, and, impatiently, she complied,

'Right.'

'So I go straight ahead and ruin them both. End of story. Why would I go to the extent of saddling myself with a wildcat wife when I could go out and find myself a nice tame pussy-cat?'

He took an appreciative mouthful from his glass and arched her a look that challenged her to come up with an answer. And she was wondering how to tell him that she'd already worked that one out, knew it was another humiliating twist in his search for revenge without letting him know that she actually minded that he didn't even want her sexually, when he blocked that train of thought entirely with the unexpected—yet again.

'And can you honestly believe that my father would have come to me for financial help and advice if I'd been plotting revenge all my life? If I'd truly resented being illegitimate, envied his regular family and their life together to that extent, it would have shown. Don't forget, he and I met up at frequent and regular intervals since I was a child. He would have known. You can't hide feelings of that kind. I repeat, he would have known. And, knowing, he wouldn't even have hinted at his financial troubles. He's not a fool.'

She stared at him, trying to take it all in. Everything he had said bore the stamp of logic. She sucked at the corner of her lower lip, her golden eyes bewildered, her voice thin and thready as she demanded again, 'Then why the blackmail? I don't understand. Why involve me?'

'Put that fertile imagination to use again, sweetheart.' He was smiling, like a tiger, and the movements of his black-clad body were feline, supremely elegant, as he moved towards her. And she was too muddled and confused by his clever tongue, the logical reasoning he'd tossed her way to offer even a token protest when he took her arms and lifted her to her feet.

He had turned what she had known, what she had figured out all by herself, right on its head. The situation was unreal, made so by this plausible devil. And her crazy heart was hammering as if there was no tomorrow, beating against her ribs in a frenzy as he held her immobile within the warm circle of his arms, his taut body just touching hers, the tenuous, tormenting contact making her flesh leap in helpless, hopeless response, overriding the frantic warnings of her brain.

She could no more control her response to him than a flower could resist opening in the rays of the sun, and, as his lips descended, her own parted, soft, vulnerable, quivering with the need only he could bring to life. And disappointment rocked her where she stood as he merely brushed her mouth with cool uninterest, telling her dismissively, 'Get some sleep. You've had a hectic day. Things could seem clearer in the morning.'

She couldn't make an answer. Shame that her body should yearn so for his kisses, his devastating caresses warred with the pain of knowing he was totally indifferent. She didn't understand herself, or him. Didn't understand what was going on in her life. And, what was worse, she didn't think she ever would.

Plodding dutifully to the door, she felt his eyes burning into her back and swallowed a frustrated sob. If the situation was as unreal as she felt it to be, she would wake in the morning and find it had been nothing more than a particularly horrid nightmare.

CHAPTER EIGHT

'HELL!' The suitcase had burst open, spilling its contents over Adam's doorstep. Selina ground her teeth together in temper, the accident not improving a mood that had grown from bad to worse over the last ten days.

Not that she could blame her bleak irritability on Adam. Since he had forced her to move in with him she had seen very little of him—supper together on the three evenings when he'd returned before midnight and breakfast each morning. And on all of these occasions he'd behaved impeccably, enquiring about her day, sometimes telling her about his, asking whether she'd phoned Martin—which, of course, she always had—and never once referring to the marriage which hung over her like a huge black cloud, never once attempting to touch her, to kiss her.

Which was exactly what she wanted, wasn't it? If their future together was to run along such cool, polite tracks then she would be grateful for small mercies, wouldn't she?

Cursing the faulty fastenings on her suitcase, the persistent drizzle falling from the black night sky, she pushed the doorkey into her handbag again and bent to thrust the tumbled garments back into the case.

Was Adam home? Probably not. His car, behind which she'd drawn up her Volvo, was here on the cobbled mews courtyard but that meant nothing. He usually took a taxi when he was out for the evening, especially if he was dining. So, being a Saturday, he was probably out on the razzle, she decided dourly.

And she'd better get used to not knowing his whereabouts, hadn't she? He wouldn't change the habits of a lifetime after he'd forced her to make the supreme sacrifice of marrying him! Bending to retrieve a slinky satin teddy which had somehow got draped over one of the cyclamen tubs, she felt her head begin to throb. It had been a hell of a day.

For the past week and a half she'd been swamped under a spate of work, staying late at head office most days, unable to find the time to get back home to collect her car and extra clothes. She'd sent her secretary out to buy necessities—underwear, a couple of inexpensive skirts and tops—then put her head down, intent on clearing the sudden avalanche of work, only finding time to phone each day to speak to Martin.

He had been back at the Hall for a week now and he'd told her he'd broken the news of her forthcoming wedding to Adam. Vanessa, he'd confided, hadn't said much—one way or the other.

But she'd said plenty today.

Selina drew her brows together in a scowl as she thrust the last of the scattered clothing into the case and pushed down the top.

Her desk finally cleared, she had taken a taxi to Lower Otterley, looking forward to a day's respite from the strain of sharing Adam's home. But Vanessa had met her as she'd been walking through the hall, her features frozen, as if carved from marble.

'I'm surprised you managed to tear yourself away from your fiancé to visit your uncle.' That was for openers and Selina couldn't tell her the truth—that sharing Adam's home wasn't her idea of a picnic, that she would much prefer to be back here, back home, where she knew who she was, where she was going. To do so would highlight all those lies she'd told about falling in love.

So Selina followed meekly into the drawing-room when Vanessa said crisply, 'I want a word with you before you see Martin.'

But Vanessa said nothing for long, taut moments, going to stand in front of the fire, holding her thin hands out to the flames, her back rigid beneath the soft wool of her long-sleeved, aubergine-coloured sheath dress.

'Well?' Selina asked quietly at last, unable to stand the tension any longer, her face paling as her aunt turned slowly and she felt the full force of the waves of antagonism coming from the older woman.

'Well, indeed.' Her aunt was still a beautiful woman, with her bone-structure she would look lovely at any age, but her features were marred by an icy temper only just kept under control. 'I hope you know what you're doing? I've always done my best for you, brought you up as if you were my own daughter. And you repay me by stabbing me in the back!'

'Oh, but how?' Selina asked dulcetly, remembering just in time that she had to behave as if she were a woman in love and therefore inclined to see the world through a rosy glow. 'I'd never deliberately set out to hurt anyone, you know that—especially not you and Martin.'

'Don't put on a sweetness-and-light act with me!' Vanessa riposted with a dismissive jerk of her head. 'You know who that man is, what he is, yet apparently you intend marrying him!' She walked over to the drinks cabinet, her movements oddly uncoordinated, and poured herself a Scotch.

Selina's eyes widened. Except for special occasions, Vanessa never touched alcohol until the evening, and then only a pre-dinner sherry with Martin, a single glass of wine with her meal.

'We love each other.' Selina had to force herself to defend herself with that lie. Martin must never get to know the truth. But her throat closed on the unpalatable untruth, her voice emerging chokily, and Vanessa gave a humourless laugh.

'Love? Him? He won't know the meaning of the word!' And Selina's inner admission that her aunt was absolutely right was, unaccountably, like a physical pain. He had admitted that much himself. In that, at least, he had been honest.

Vanessa took a long swallow of whisky, set the glass aside and shuddered then shot Selina an accusing glance as if she was responsible for the uncharacteristic intake of neat spirits. And she said, as if the alcohol had coarsened her tongue, 'He's a handsome devil, I'll give you that. But for God's sake, Selina, if you've got the hots for him then go ahead, sleep with him, get it out of your system. But for pity's sake don't marry the bastard! Think with your head instead of your hormones—his mother was scheming, cold-blooded and calculating, and she handed her genes on to her son, with interest!' She dragged in a breath, as if to calm herself, yet her voice still shook with rage as she added, 'Martin finally told me how much we're in hock to the creep. If I'd had an inkling of what was in the wind I wouldn't have allowed it to happen. As it is, he can and he will ruin the lot of us. Do you want to be a party to that? As his wife, you'll be tarred with the same devil's brush!'

But only by becoming his wife could she stop the ruin Vanessa was prophesying, but she couldn't admit to that.

Her aunt might reluctantly agree to such a sacrifice but Martin wouldn't.

Selina shivered; she could share the bleak prospects of her future with no one and, although she hadn't expected Vanessa to be over the moon about the forthcoming wedding, she hadn't expected such a bitter tongue-lashing. And whether it was her aunt's spiteful reference to her hormones or her character-blackening remarks about Adam she didn't know, but, whatever, she felt her own temper rising to boiling-point and had to summon all her self-control to keep her tone level as she pointed out, 'I'm marrying Adam, with your blessing or without it, so why don't you try to make the best of it, as Uncle's managed to?' She tilted her head proudly, her eyes cold. 'And I can give you my assurance that he'll do nothing to harm you financially.'

That assurance was all she could offer, and it was as bitter as gall. And the sudden hurt, the black hopelessness of it all, seemed too much to bear, making her ask with uncharacteristic spite, 'And while we're on the subject of people ruining other people—when's Dominic going to come out of hiding and get back to work? Or has Adam given him the boot?' then wished she'd stayed silent when she saw the dull red stain cover her aunt's face.

But she bit back the impulsive apology, remembering all those times Vanessa had taken Dom's word against hers, when she'd gone out of her way to let her, Selina, know that although she was welcome to a home she would never be part of the family, that as far as her aunt was concerned she was here under sufferance, like a stray with no place else to go.

So the apology was left unspoken as Selina swung on her heel and walked out of the room. Taking refuge with

Martin in his sitting-room, she spent the morning with him, playing chess with the jade pieces she remembered she'd found for his birthday, taking a trouncing because she couldn't concentrate. And after the light lunch Meg had prepared, over which Vanessa had been coldly polite, she'd taken time and care over packing her clothes, only to have them tumble on to the wet cobblestones!

Gingerly testing the fastenings, she fished the key Adam had given her out of the depths of her bag and turned it in the door, and was dragging her case up the stairs when he snapped from behind her, 'Where the hell do you think you've been?'

'Where do you think?' she snapped right back, stung by his tone, her bad mood translating into sheer, bloody-minded temper. 'You don't own me yet, so don't try to act as if you do!'

'I'm not trying,' he answered shortly, his mouth thin, his magnificent eyes punishing her. 'I do own you, and you know it.'

And that was her misfortune, and suddenly, after the uneasy calm of the last ten days, it was too much to bear with dignity and, her mouth white with temper, she yelled down at him, 'You don't, and you won't. Not ever!' And she had two seconds in which to mourn her loss of poise, the coolness she had promised herself would be the hallmark of all her dealings with him, before he had mounted the stairs, taking the suitcase from her and hurling it to the head of the staircase in one violent movement.

Then he dragged her up, setting her down on the landing with a thud beside the suitcase which, miraculously, was still intact. And before she could get sufficient breath back to demand to know what he thought he was doing he rasped, 'I've been going out of my mind all day, wondering where you were. Dammit, for all I knew you could have fallen under a bus!'

'I should be so lucky!' she sniped, then closed her eyes, appalled by hitherto unsuspected fishwife tendencies. He brought things out of her she hadn't known were there. And he had looked as if he'd meant every word, as if he had been worried about her, and she said in a thready whisper, 'I'm sorry. You hadn't surfaced when I left but I should have written a note. I went to collect my car and some clothes. You might have guessed. You should have phoned to check, if you really were anxious.'

'And let them see a chink in our united façade?' he enquired with slow scorn. 'The besotted couple coming adrift, one of them not knowing where the other is?'

Clearly, he was far from mollified and, not really knowing why she should bother, she appeased, 'Don't let's argue.' She didn't like the cynical gleam in his eyes but ploughed doggedly on. 'I've had the sort of day I'd rather forget. Apart from being bad-mouthed by Vanessa, my suitcase burst and everything's covered in mud.'

She didn't add that she had been getting more and more wound up for the past ten days, that living with him, having him treat her like a stranger he had no inclination to get to know better had been like slow torture. She didn't tell him because she didn't know why this should be. And he just might.

Terse eyes flickered over her then crinkled at the corners, his mouth a teasing lilt as he told her, 'Quite a day! Sort out what needs washing and we'll put it in the machine. And I'll fix something to eat. Unless you'd rather go out?'

Turning out again into the damp dark drizzle didn't appeal. She shook her head.

'I'd rather stay put. But don't let me stop you.'

'You won't, I promise.' Laughter lurked in the caressing curl of his voice as he bent to pick up her case, carrying it through to her bedroom and placing it at the foot of the bed. And she followed, her feet dragging.

She didn't trust him when he appeared to be sharing jokes with himself. Or when he was treating her like a human being when for the last ten days she might have been a piece of furniture. She didn't trust him, full stop.

But she didn't trust herself when he was in the bedroom with her, when his beautiful mouth was curved in the wicked smile that was unique to him, when the olive-green fine wool sweater he wore tempted her fingers to touch that magnificent torso. No, she didn't trust her crazy, irrational, hormonal responses one little bit. So she remained stiffly by the door, making her face wooden, and he grinned at her, suddenly, with enough charm to stop an exocet in its tracks, and walked towards her, past her, pausing only to slide a forefinger down the elegant length of her nose, murmuring, 'Supper in half an hour, sweetheart. And don't worry. It will be all right on the night, I promise!'

He closed the door gently behind him and she stared into space, rigid as a rock. She hated it when she didn't know what he meant, when he talked in innuendoes which could be translated to carry a sexual content.

Giving herself a mental shake, she made herself unpack her case, putting aside the things that would need to be washed—surprisingly few, considering—selecting fresh underwear and her favourite relaxing-in housecoat, decently ankle-length and, when tightly belted, high at the cross-over neckline; then she went through to shower.

She would not do as the new-found cowardly streak in her prompted: stay in her room pleading a sick headache, extricating herself from supper for two, a whole evening for two if she read the signs aright. If he was planning to tease her a little, bone up on his ability to arouse her again to the point of wanton capitulation, then drop her like a red-hot coal, he would learn what it was like to be on the receiving end of rejection.

She had learnt the hard way, but she now knew how to handle him.

But an hour later she wasn't so sure. Not that he'd tried anything; it wasn't that. He hadn't even touched her, except with his eyes. But that slow, drifting, caressing inspection had had more impact than a full-blooded, hand-roving embrace from any other man could possibly have done.

As on her first night here, they'd eaten from the coffee-table in the sitting-room. He'd made a simple meal of scrambled eggs and grilled mushrooms, with cheese and fresh fruit to follow, and his attitude, again, had changed. He was treating her like his best buddy.

It was that she didn't know how to handle, she confessed to herself as she insisted on making the coffee as her contribution to the meal. Waiting for it to perc, she leant against the stainless-steel units and wondered why she should feel so relaxed yet, at one and the same time, perversely uneasy.

By the time she carried the tray through she had her answer. He was treating her as though she were a valued platonic friend, talking to her as if she had a mind of her own, actually had a brain in working order. And she had responded on the same level, opening up, relaxing, discovering that they held much the same views on topics as divergent as world politics, music and literature—even supporting the same charity. And because of that she actually found herself liking the man!

Liking him, respecting his views, was not on her agenda. Definitely not! So how was she supposed to handle it?

By constantly reminding herself of what a louse he really was, she told herself firmly as she carried the tray through.

But the 'louse' had shared the last of the wine between their two glasses and he rose at once to take the tray from her, pouring, setting her cup in front of her and taking the wind out of her sails yet again by asking, 'What did Vanessa say to upset you?'

It took her a moment or two, her eyes following the movements of his strong-boned hands as he stirred his coffee, to recall that she'd told him earlier that her aunt had bad-mouthed her, thereby contributing to her own grumpy mood.

'What do you think?' she tossed back with a wry smile, an elegant shrug of satin-covered shoulders, and his own mouth curved ironically.

'That she didn't go a bundle on the idea of our marrying?'

'You got it!' Slumbrous golden eyes smiled into the green of his and she felt herself begin to melt inside, cherishing the warmth she found in those translucent depths, and the whole world shrank to the space of one room, the two of them, together, cocooned in the gentle embrace of complete intimacy.

And she had to shake her head to make herself concentrate on what he was telling her, his voice lazy, as if nothing could be bad enough, harsh enough, to shatter this precious mood of soft rapport.

'It's to be expected, but don't let it get to you. She'll come round eventually.' He settled further back in his chair, one long leg hooked over the other, his eyes veiled by those incredibly long, thick dark lashes. 'She's always bitterly resented my existence, got insanely jealous at the thought of my father having anything to do with me, apart from sending regular maintenance cheques. Which was why our meetings always had to be kept secret, unfortunately.'

'Didn't you mind?' Selina asked without thinking. Of course he had minded, still did, must do, because if he hadn't cared he wouldn't have come up with this twisted blackmail idea. But he shook his head, his slow smile almost convincing her that she might have been mistaken—as he had told her she was—about his need for revenge.

'No. I didn't grow up with any hang-ups.' He steepled his long hands, fingertips resting against his clear-cut mouth as he added reflectively, 'That's not quite true. When I was around nine or ten years old I began to resent the fact that my father only appeared occasionally, that he would play with me, talk to me, and then disappear for weeks on end. I got pretty troublesome around that time.' Then his eyes crinkled at the corners in the slow, intimate smile that made Selina feel weak all over.

Quickly, she poured herself fresh coffee and sipped the scalding liquid, punishing herself for her mindless response to him, and he said consideringly, 'We're alike in a lot of ways, you and I. We both know what we want from life and go right out and get it. And the reason we're both emotionally unattached is, primarily, because we don't really feel secure. Your parents died, which is a form of rejection, you felt abandoned—passed on like a stray dog who needed a new home. And, as I was just explaining, early on I felt rejected, too, until my mother realised why I was playing up and taught me better.' He leaned forward, holding her with his eyes. 'She told me that my father was proud of me, loved me deeply. But he didn't love her—at least, not in the way he loved Vanessa. And, that being so, his place was with Vanessa but he came to see me just as often as he could, and thought about me all the time. After that I began to come to terms with only seeing my father occasionally, and I got to know him better through the long letters he wrote every week.' He grinned at her. 'Much later on, that's how I got to know all about you—through his letters—how you had come to live with them, how courageous and spunky you were, how you were getting on at school, how you punched Dominic and gave him a black eye because he'd pulled up all the flowers you'd grown in your own patch of garden. So many things, over the span of years. You brought joy to his life in so many ways.'

His eyes softened until they were like pools of limpid green water, and she couldn't look away, until he said gently, 'I think his uncomplicated enjoyment of your staunch little character infected me. I felt your charisma, even before I met you.'

It was too much to take on board, too much to think about right now. She would need time on her own to come to terms with all he'd said. With conscious effort, she tore her eyes from his steady, almost mesmeric gaze and, swallowing the last of her wine, she picked out the one safe thread in the fabric of his confidences and asked with carefully assumed concern, 'Talking of Dominic—have you seen him? Is he coming back to work? And when?'

If he was disappointed because she had ignored the insight he had given her into his early relationship with Martin, his confession—for what it was worth—that he'd followed the details of her life with more than a passing interest, she would never know. She didn't trust herself to look at him and discover whatever truth there was to be discovered.

She kept her eyes on her fingers, laced together on her knees. But his tone was perfectly level, telling her nothing at all as he replied, 'I've seen him. I gave him a few days off to come to terms with the fact that he'll be paying back every penny of the money he "borrowed" out of his salary. He'll be short of pocket money for the next ten years. And he'll be in his office on Monday, his nose to the grindstone with a vengeance.' He got to his feet and Selina glanced at him warily, sensing his mood change. 'I don't think he'll err in that direction again. He knows what's coming to him if he does.'

His eyes were cold, like splinters of green stone. Selina met them and looked quickly away. She wouldn't like to be his enemy. She shivered helplessly, and he advised her tonelessly, 'Layers of heavy woollies might not be as glamorous as that pulse-raiser of a thing you're wearing, but they sure as hell keep the cold out.' He swung away. 'If you'll excuse me, I've work to do in my room. I shan't see you again tonight, so why don't you dress in something warmer to help you stop shuddering with the cold?'

CHAPTER NINE

SHE should have worn the satin robe. She was far too hot and the soft, slinky fabric felt cool against her heated skin—sensuous, erotic. If she'd been wearing it, would Adam have taken it off, sliding it away from her body, trailing his long fingers over her aroused flesh, made love to her?

No, no, of course he wouldn't. Selina thrashed her head against the pillow. She saw his face, very close. Lean, the hard-cut features austere, his eyes contemptuous, disgusted. Despite all his honeyed words, when push came to shove he didn't want her. Never had, never would. As far as he was concerned, she was a turn-off. But she should have worn the satin robe...

Pushing against the tightly cocooning duvet, her naked arms found freedom, and as the cool air brushed against her burning skin the muddled dream-thoughts slipped away and she slid down to deeper, restful sleep only to hear that sexy voice say her name. Say it again.

Her eyelids fluttered, and she felt the burning brand of his palm against the cool skin of her shoulder, his fingers tightening as he gave her a gentle shake, his voice warm and dark as he instructed, 'Wake up, sweetheart. We're going out.'

Out? She struggled up against the pillows, her eyes winging open as she saw him standing over her. He looked rugged and dangerous in dark brown, narrow-fitting cords, a black wool shirt tucked into the lean waistband. And for a moment she panicked. Had she overslept so badly, been due in at work hours ago? Then she recalled that today was Sunday and the golden haze of her eyes cleared and sharpened to pin-points of light as she sat up higher, running her tongue over her lips to moisten them.

'What did you say?' He had never come into her room, never come near it since he'd shown her where she was to sleep, and if he was planning on tormenting her, sipping a little deeper from the cup of revenge ...

She stiffened her backbone, instinctively readying herself to counter an attack from whatever angle he chose to mount it, hoisting up the slender strap that kept the fine silk, scoopy top of her nightdress in place. And saw his eyes harden as they followed the movement—harden with disgust? Revulsion?

He swung away, crossing the room to fling back the curtains, his back still to her as he repeated, 'We're going out. It's a beautiful morning and there's something I want to show you.'

Clear winter sunlight flooded into the room and Selina pulled the duvet up to her chin, hunching back against the pillows, her cheeks going pink. He obviously thought she'd been flaunting herself, asking him to fondle the warm, full breasts so inadequately covered by the clinging, almost transparent cream silk, inviting him to——

That look of revulsion still haunted her and her voice was sharp and clear as he walked to the door.

'And what if I don't want to go?'

He ignored that small rebellion, his face expressionless as he turned briefly to face her.

'Dress in something warm and comfortable. And don't take all day about it.'

Selina pulled a face at the door as he closed it behind him. So much for any plans she might have made. It was a case of 'Do as I say, or else.' He could make her jump through hoops if he wanted to. As long as he had the power to ruin Martin she had no will of her own.

And yet he had spoken fondly of his father last night. And she could still feel the savage bite of his anger when he'd discovered how she'd kept the facts of Martin's illness from him. So many things didn't add up, didn't make sense.

Despite his terse injunction, she took her time, choosing to take a bath instead of a shower, her mind occupied with the enigma that was Adam Tudor.

If he was sincere in his affection for Martin why would he even contemplate his ruination? And if she was supposed to believe what he'd told her—that he felt it was time he married, had children—then why pick a wife he didn't want to make love to?

Someone was lying. And it had to be Adam.

And no amount of struggling to find answers to the riddles would alter the fact that, whatever happened, she was going to have to marry him because she couldn't just wash her hands of the whole affair and watch Martin lose everything.

Aware at last that the water was cooling uncomfortably, she scrambled out and reached for a fluffy bath-sheet from one of the heated rails. And as she huddled in the warm and comforting folds she admitted in a moment of shocking self-knowledge that, had the sexual chemistry that worked so potently for her afflicted him, too, then, despite the fact that they didn't love each other, she would have been looking forward to the wedding, to belonging to him, to the task of making the marriage work, building on mutual sexual attraction, respect and liking.

But how could she like or respect a man who would stoop to blackmail, who threatened to ruin his own father if he didn't get what he wanted? Which brought her round full circle to the stumbling-block of his contempt and disgust. He knew how easily he could arouse her sexually and that disgusted him. She'd seen the contempt in his eyes when he'd thrust her away from him because he couldn't stomach the thought of taking their lovemaking to its logical conclusion.

What was it he wanted from her?

Straightening her backbone, she informed herself that she was wasting her time trying to sort things out in her head. Adam would never come clean and tell her; he was playing her just as a cat tormented a mouse—and enjoying it. And the answer wouldn't come out of thin air, so, to avoid becoming hopelessly agitated, she would have to get on with her life as best she could. And that meant spending the day with him, because he had said she must. So she would. But her compliance didn't mean she would have to enjoy it.

Taking her cue from him, she dressed in a warm tweed skirt in a shade of burnt red, leather boots and a loose cream wool sweater, tortured her springy mane of tawny hair into a single thick braid and, apart from a smear of moisturiser and a slick of soft rose lipstick, eschewed make-up and was as ready as she would ever be.

Firmly suppressing all curiosity about the day ahead, she walked into the kitchen and found him closing the lid of a wicker hamper. A picnic? In January? But she wasn't going to ask. He was calling all the shots, making the arrangements, and she was having to go along with him, whether she wanted to or not. A complete lack of interest was the only civilised way she could show her opposition, she decided stubbornly.

'There's tea in the pot, if you want it.' The hint of tautness in his voice, in the set of the wide shoulders beneath the soft leather jacket he now wore over the black wool shirt was the only indication of his displeasure over the amount of time she had taken to get ready.

Selina merely shrugged and determinedly made a slice of toast and ate it at the breakfast bar, sipping her way through two cups of tea as he carried the hamper out to the car then came back, leaning against the kitchen door, the car keys jingling in his hands as she slowly finished the breakfast she hadn't wanted in the first place.

'If you're trying to annoy me, you're failing,' he remarked conversationally, a smile on his mouth as she set her cup back on its saucer. But the smile didn't reach those glacial green eyes, so she knew he was lying, that, for some reason, the day he had planned was important to him.

Suddenly feeling ashamed of herself for her childish obstinacy, she walked past him to the hall, reaching for her own leather jacket from the cupboard, annoyed that she should be ashamed, that she should consider his feelings at all when he clearly never gave hers a second thought.

And it was a lovely day, she conceded as they drove out of London. The sky was cloudless, a clear harsh blue, the air crisp and still, a gift from the gods in a winter that had been disgusting so far. And it was stupid to sulk, to answer his conversational openers with grunts and shrugs, to pretend an interest in the boring discussion on a dreary subject that was coming from the car radio which she'd turned on the moment she'd settled in her seat.

She turned it off and glanced at his impassive profile and saw his lips twitch when she asked, 'Where are we going?' as if he had known it had only been a matter of time before she gave in to her natural curiosity.

'The Cotswolds,' he told her and, before she could ask more, went on, 'I had thought we could visit Martin together today, but that will have to wait.'

'Vanessa would have been pleased!' The slight sarcasm in her voice was overlaid by a tremor of unease. She had always been much closer to her uncle than to her aunt, but, in her own cool way, Vanessa had been good to her and she would always be grateful.

'Don't worry about it. Vanessa will accept me as part of the family eventually.' His tone was dry and Selina countered impulsively, without thinking, 'Is that why you're insisting on our marriage? To force your way into the family that shut you out for nearly forty years?' But even as she was speaking she knew that simply couldn't be true. His character was too forceful, too compelling and ruthless for him to be that insecure, and without even looking at him she could feel the lazy smile on that beautifully shaped mouth as he said,

'Get real, sweetheart! You know exactly why we're marrying. I explained it quite succinctly at the time, as I recall.'

But not succinctly enough, she thought, chewing on her bottom lip. Words were meaningless when actions spoke louder. He didn't desire her, as he had claimed. He was always the one to back off, that shaming look of contempt in his eyes, he was the one who had forced her to live with him, adding an embarrassing veracity to the lies she had told about their passionate love for each other. Yet during most of the time she'd spent at his home he had treated her as if she were invisible.

Unconsciously, she shook her head. She would probably go to her grave without ever fathoming his true reasons.

But he was saying, 'Don't be too hard on Vanessa for her opposition to our marriage. As far as she's concerned, I'm poison. But you know that, of course. When our meeting became inevitable she made sure you knew I was poison, too. True?' He took his eyes off the motorway for long enough to glint down into her eyes and she nodded briefly, her own eyes dropping to the lean, hard hands that were so confident on the wheel, as he told her, 'In a way, it's difficult to blame her. My mother and Martin told me enough to explain the way she feels. Apparently, my father met and fell instantly and deeply in love with Vanessa before he knew my mother was pregnant. When she did write and tell him, Martin was appalled. Not only was he morally and physically responsible, but he had met the woman he knew he would love all his life, the woman who had agreed to marry him, even though they had known each other for a matter of mere weeks.

'He did the only thing he could, and made his confession to his fiancée. Naturally, she was hurt and angry, but eventually forgave him because the affair had happened before they'd met.' His voice took on the dry tone she now knew hid deep feelings. 'The affair, incidentally, lasted for one night only. But with the forgiveness came conditions. Martin had to promise never to see either my mother or myself, that the monthly maintenance payments, made through a solicitor, were to be the only contact.'

'A promise Martin broke,' Selina mused. 'Did Vanessa know?'

'I believe not. And you know, when my mother told me this, it helped. That my father had broken his promise to the woman he adored, because he needed to have contact with me, gave me a feeling of security, of importance, that I'll never forget. It was a good sensation for a bolshie ten-year-old to have.' He shot her his blindingly charismatic smile, sending an intense shiver running down her spine, then added soberly, 'But things weren't going well for Vanessa. She had three miscarriages before Dominic was born, ten years into their marriage. And each time that happened the trauma was heightened by the knowledge that I existed, that Martin already had a living, healthy son. It must have been more than tough on her. And, naturally enough, I suppose, when she gave birth to a son she wrapped him in cotton wool. As far as she was concerned, Dominic could do no wrong.'

'So that's why she spoiled him rotten.' Selina was at last beginning to understand why Vanessa was blinkered as far as her only, beloved son was concerned. She hadn't known about those early miscarriages. Vanessa never took her into her confidence over anything that really mattered to her.

And Adam affirmed, 'Too true. And that brings me to my feelings of guilt. If I hadn't handled things badly, Martin might not have had that attack.'

She shot him a narrow-eyed glance. Had her aunt and cousin been right all along—had Martin been terrified of a meeting with Adam, knowing he could—and probably would—ruin him? For all his earlier professed fondness of and closeness to his father, was he now admitting that he was indeed his enemy?

But Adam told her heavily, 'It was Martin who first suspected that money was going astray. He knew Dominic's salary, of course, and he knew he was living way above his means. To cut a long story short, the discrepancies were easily traced and we'd arranged that if what we suspected was true I'd call at the Hall to face Dominic with what we knew.' He dragged air into his lungs, the sound short and sharp. 'When he got my message he knew what was coming. He had already faced it in his own mind but what really stressed him was the thought of having to tell Vanessa that their son was a thief. Not only that, he was going to have to confess my bank's interest in the matter. I'm convinced that the anxiety over Vanessa's possible reaction brought on the attack. I should have arranged things differently, hauled Dominic into my office.' His voice was terse with regret. 'But Martin insisted that a more informal meeting, at the Hall, keeping everything private and trying to sort out the mess without the bank having to prosecute, was the best way. I shouldn't have listened. I should have realised what the stress of the situation could do.'

'You handled the affair the way Martin believed best,' Selina pointed out unevenly. 'And he's going to be OK. Is OK. Right?' She felt shattered. Was shattered. Whatever he had said, she now knew that whatever happened he could no more ruin his father, take away all he had ever worked for, than fly to the moon on the back of a bat! His sincere affection for Martin, going back so many years, simply wouldn't let him.

The sense of release was incredible, and the joy of knowing he wasn't the ruthless bastard he had pretended to be was almost a pain, deep within her.

She turned to look out of the window, hiding the sudden spring of tears in her eyes. They had left the motorway behind them, bypassing Gloucester, heading for the hills through lanes which grew ever narrower, taking them through quaint old villages and past occasional stone manor houses with their mullioned windows glittering like diamonds in the morning sunlight.

His threats had meant nothing, nothing at all.

They weren't married, and no real arrangements had been made to that end. And yet, far from having his half-brother flung in gaol, publicly disgraced, he had worked something out, tough but fair—and better than Dominic deserved. She could refuse point blank to contemplate marrying him, safe in the knowledge that he would do nothing to harm the family or the business.

So why wasn't she telling him just that? Why had reluctance frozen her tongue? And why wasn't she filled with righteous anger because he'd had her jumping like a puppet on a string, dancing to his tune of blackmail, cowed and cornered by threats she now knew he had no intention of carrying out?

Nothing, absolutely nothing made sense any more. Not even her own reactions to the shattering conviction that she was free. Free as a bird.

She was preoccupied with her own thoughts, but a tiny part of her mind registered that they had turned off the metalled surface of the lane and were now on what amounted to little more than a track which wound through a valley enclosed by gentle, tree-clad hills. And Adam broke the silence.

'Almost there.'

'Where?' Her response was automatic, wooden. She had ceased caring about their destination when she'd started wondering what he was up to, what devious plans he'd been hatching when he'd made those empty threats.

'Home.' The single word was spoken with pride, a certain affection, but, like everything he said, it was ambiguous. His home, as she knew only too well, was in London. Did he mean that he intended they should live around here after their marriage?

Marriage? Why on earth was she still thinking in those terms when she could, quite safely, tell him to get lost? And why the aching regret? She couldn't really want him to force her into the most intimate relationship two people could share, could she?

Her thoughts were too self-revealing, too uncomfortable to tolerate, so when the dwelling came into view, around the final bend in the track, she put her attention on it and held it there.

It wasn't a large house, but its mellow stone sturdiness impressed her. It looked secure, welcoming, and somehow familiar, nestled as it was in the crook of the hills that enclosed the high valley. Home. Yes, it looked like a real home.

'It's nice,' she said inadequately as Adam parked the car in front of stone gateposts, behind which were the remains of a once cultivated garden. He dipped his head briefly, a wry acknowledgement of her guarded response, and told her, 'Martin bought it for my mother when he knew I was on the way. She couldn't stay on where she was and he insisted on finding a home she'd be happy in. She chose this place and he gave it to her. I spent the first eighteen years of my life here. After she died, it came to me.'

'And was she happy here?' Selina couldn't help asking, a tiny frown furrowing her brow. How could a woman as allegedly promiscuous as she, a slave to her sex drive, have been happy in such an isolated situation?

'She was content.'

His answer puzzled her. Vanessa had said that Adam's mother had been scheming, cold-blooded and calculating; could she have settled for contentment?

She didn't suppose she would ever know and agreed readily enough when Adam suggested, 'Shall we stretch our legs, get some real fresh air into our lungs, before we go inside?'

She fell in step beside him as he took a track that ran from the side of the house, deeper into the silent valley. Breathing deeply, she felt pure, clean air tingle into her lungs and decided to enjoy the day, the surroundings, and forget the riddles, the feeling that if only she could find a way through the layers of equivocation that surrounded Adam Tudor she would find, at last, the essential man.

The conviction that she was beginning to do so tormented her. She was no nearer guessing his motives than she had been ten days ago, further away, in actuality, because then it had seemed as clear-cut as anything as murky as blackmail could be.

Annoyed with herself for allowing him and his motives to occupy her mind when she had, moments ago, determined she wouldn't, she lengthened her swinging stride and looked around her.

The dead-time, winter-bare valley should have been depressing. But, strangely, it wasn't. Maybe it was the sparkling blue sky, the rough warmth encapsulated within the bark of the skeletal trees, the pale ochre of dead grass. Subtle, achingly tender colour was everywhere she looked, promising the rebirth of springtime, so maybe that was why she suddenly felt ecstatically, foolishly happy. It was nothing at all to do with the way he reached out for her hand to steady her as the path suddenly dipped downwards and sideways across a rocky scree.

'We're heading back now,' he told her as the ground levelled out and the track curled round to wander through low scrub. 'Another twenty minutes should see us back at the house. I'll get a fire going while you make coffee.'

That sounded good. And she wasn't objecting to the way he had kept possession of her hand, holding it firmly in his, tucking it beneath his arm so that as they walked she could feel the brush of his thighs against her own. It felt right.

Selina was letting go, pushing her problematic relationship with this man right out of her mind, and by the time they reached the little house she was completely relaxed, feeling good, her skin glowing with the exercise in the fresh, cold air.

He steered her to the kitchen. 'First things first,' he told her as he turned on electricity and water. 'If you ferret around you'll find the makings of coffee. I'll get the fire going.' And he disappeared through an outer door to return just as she'd put the kettle to boil with an armful of split logs and kindling.

'You suit the place.' He flashed her the charismatic grin that made his austerely carved features totally irresistible and disappeared into the sitting-room, leaving her feeling unexpectedly disorientated as she took stock of her surroundings.

The quarry-tiled kitchen was large, obviously doubling as living and eating space, the Victorian pine cupboards and table, the Windsor chairs and pretty scarlet curtains making it homey. Could he really see her here, all domesticated, ministering to his needs, with the old-fashioned black-leaded range alight and glowing as she bustled round baking, preparing his favourite casseroles, just the two of them in this hidden seclusion?

Selina briskly put the idea right out of play. She was a career woman, she reminded herself. Barely domesticated. Furthermore, the idea of her and Adam as a couple was ridiculous. The leverage he had claimed was false.

So why the ridiculous pang of regret? He didn't even want her physically. He had effectively proved that. He was merely playing with her, making up the rules in a devious game of his own devising.

And that the sheer power of her desire for him should make her a willing wanton whenever he took her in his arms was just her bad luck. But she would get over it, she assured herself. Lust didn't last; how could it? The sooner she moved out of his life, the better.

She couldn't imagine why she hadn't stated her intention to do just that as soon as she'd realised he'd been bluffing. Give her a couple of weeks without seeing him and she'd forget he existed.

As soon as the thought was formed she knew she was lying to herself. He was a man she'd find it impossible to forget. But that truth was too depressing for words.

Firming her mouth, she grabbed the two mugs of coffee and stomped through to the sitting-room. But all her icy intentions to let him know she was moving out of his orbit forthwith, daring him to go ahead and ruin his own father, melted away in the sheer warmth of the green eyes that smiled into hers as he stood up from the hearth. And the all too familiar weakness sapped her strength as his fingers brushed hers when he took one of the mugs.

She was a fool, she told herself, lowering her eyes to hide the self-castigation that was going on inside her head and, seeing him settle his booted feet on the lushly piled rug in front of the crackling log fire, she cradled her mug in her hands and walked into the body of the room, making herself take an interest to divert her attention from him.

His town house was expensively furnished, but impersonal. This was different. The cottage antiques were fine quality, each piece obviously chosen with care, lovingly tended. But it was the series of framed watercolours that drew her eye, distracting her momentarily from his vital, disturbing presence.

They were executed in the same exquisitely simple style as the one on his wall back in town—the painting depicting this house, this valley, she realised, knowing now why she had felt the place to be vaguely familiar. And the signature at the bottom of each of the paintings was the same. Ellen Tudor.

'My mother.'

Selina jumped wildly. He had crept up behind her and his voice, his arm draped around her shoulder, had taken her unawares, and he said softly, 'Relax, little cat. I'm not going to eat you, not just yet. What do you think of them?'

'Lovely.' The mumbled response was totally inadequate, she knew that. But she was trying to equate the calculating schemer of Vanessa's description to the woman who had painted with such loving sensitivity.

Adam said drily, 'Towards the end of her life she became respected enough as an artist to name her own price for her work. But she was too unassuming, too innocent to take it in. I wish you could have met her. She was a wonderful, warm and talented woman.'

Suddenly, achingly, Selina, too, wished she had known Ellen Tudor, and she turned bewildered eyes to him, saying unthinkingly, 'Vanessa said she was cold, a schemer—promiscuous,' and went scarlet, wishing the cruel words unspoken, but Adam merely shrugged, knowing better, his voice dry as he told her,

'Well, she would. How else could she justify her hatred of the woman who had born her husband's child? She had those miscarriages, remember, before Dominic was born, and was told she would never bear another. She had to convince herself that the mother of her husband's child was worthless; how else could she have survived those disappointments, the sense of inadequacy she must have suffered?'

Without her being aware of how it had happened, Adam had drawn her back to the hearth, helping her out of her jacket, and she flopped down on to the rug, her legs curled up beneath her, her hands held out to the warmth of the flames as the last of her misconceptions dissolved away. And she asked thickly, 'Why do you keep this place? Memories?'

'Partly.' He dropped into the armchair behind her, his knees angled on either side of her body, his hands on her shoulders, long fingers gently massaging away the tension that was beginning to gather there. 'More of a bolt-hole, really. I come here to unwind, when I get sick of the City, of power games. It renews my spirit, reinforces my ideas of what is important in life.'

The firm, caressing touch of his fingers as they kneaded the slender bones and gradually relaxing muscles of her neck and shoulders was weakening her both physically and morally. And if she didn't move now she never would.

Moving away took more effort of will than she cared to admit, but she managed it, making the excuse that the fire was too hot, taking the chair on the opposite side of the hearth. But his low, curling smile told her he didn't believe her, that he knew precisely why she had scrambled away from his touch, and she said quickly, breathily, to defuse the sexual tension she could feel spiralling so shamefully inside her, 'Can you tell me about your mother? Why didn't Martin marry her, instead of Vanessa?'

'Because he didn't love her,' he replied simply. 'Ellen always knew that, accepted it because she had no other option.' He spread his hands eloquently. 'Imagine her as she was at nineteen——' His slightly hooded eyes held hers captive, forcing her into his thoughts. 'She'd lost her own mother when she was six years old and had been brought up entirely by her father on a remote hill farm in mid-Wales. Although she never said so, my grandfather must have been a harsh, bigoted old devil. She was desperate to study art but he refused to hear of it. She had to stay home and help. Martin came on the scene. He had finished his degree course in economics and was taking a walking holiday while he waited for his results. He based himself, bed and breakfast, at my grandfather's farm. Ellen, of course, looked after him. Naturally enough, the two young people became friendly, and when Martin learned of Ellen's thwarted ambitions he offered to help, gave her his home address and told her that if she ever wanted to make a run for it he could help her find a job and a place to live and she could study art at night school.

'The offer was made out of compassion and indignation but by this time Ellen had fallen hopelessly in love. She'd known precious little kindness in her young life, certainly none from my grandfather,' he told her in a quiet voice, and Selina bit her lips.

She didn't know why he was telling her all this. She'd only opened the conversation to defuse a situation that could have got out of hand. In fact, she'd expected a curt refusal to tell her anything, an injunction to mind her own business.

'She must have had an unhappy life,' she offered weakly, but Adam gave her a strange, twisted smile, shaking his head.

'She was one of those rare people who can find happiness anywhere. But she wasn't happy on the last night of Martin's holiday. She'd been sketching in the hills, lost track of time and returned home late to prepare the evening meal. Her father had threatened to destroy all her "time-wasting daubs" if she ever neglected her real duties again. Added to that, the young man who'd shown her so much kindness and understanding was leaving the next day. She'd fallen in love with him, and he was leaving. When she met Martin coming through the yard after she'd shut up the hens for the night, she'd been crying. He asked why and she told him about the latest row with her father. He suggested a walk and again advised her to try to break free and, because she loves him and he's leaving, the tears come again. Martin tried to comfort her, and one thing led to another, and they made love.'

He got up to throw more logs on the fire, staring into the dancing flames, and he sounded world-weary as he told her, 'In real life things don't always have happy endings. Martin was ashamed of himself for what had happened. He left, renewing his offer to help if he could, got on with his life. And that included meeting Vanessa, knowing he'd found the one woman he would adore all his life. And the rest you know. I don't think Ellen ever stopped loving him. I used to see how her eyes lit up when he came here to visit me, how she hung on his every word. But she was never bitter. She had me, his son, and she had her work. It seemed to be enough.'

Enough? Did he really believe that? Was the example of his mother's lifelong love for the man who had only ever really looked on her as a friend in need of help responsible for his own determination never to let that emotion into his life?

Selina thought Ellen's story was the saddest thing she had ever heard, and that had to be responsible for the painful lump in her throat, the sting of tears behind her eyes—and nothing to do with her acceptance of Adam's utter inability to ever fall in love.

He turned from his brooding contemplation of the fire and she looked quickly away, hoping he hadn't seen the glitter of tears in her eyes, blinking them back and asking because she couldn't help herself, 'Why did you turn up at Martin's home all those years ago? You must have known Vanessa would snub you, misinterpret anything you said.'

One eyebrow arched upwards. 'She even told you that?' He shrugged. 'It was the worst error of judgement I've ever made,' he admitted wryly. 'I'd just heard I'd been accepted for university and, since Ellen had been dead for a couple of months, I needed to share the news with my father. The last time I'd spoken to him he'd told me that Vanessa was taking Dominic away on holiday. I'd tried to reach him at his office, and couldn't, so, full of youthful impatience, went to his home. I wasn't to know that something had cropped up, delaying her departure. I nearly died when she opened that door!'

So he hadn't gone there looking for charitable hand-outs, Selina brooded, and Adam suggested lightly, 'Shall we eat? We've raked over the past enough for one lifetime.' Without waiting for her reply, he walked through to the kitchen to fetch the hamper he'd brought in from the car, and Selina, watching him as he spread out a cloth on the floor, knew that today was the last they would spend together.

This morning's revelations had allowed her to see right to the heart of the man, to recognise that for him, in his own words, love was an illusion, a convenient word to justify the basic need to mate. Because of his mother's past he, subconsciously perhaps, equated love with rejection, with pain. He refused to admit it existed, ever could exist for him, using his cynicism as a wall of defence.

Yet, for all that, or maybe because of it, his personality fascinated her. He was tough and cynical, possessed of a cool, incisive mind. But, above all, he was compassionate, able to see all sides of a given situation. He made judgements, and then he made allowances—as witnessed by his defence of Vanessa, the woman who had stolen his father away from his mother.

Because that was what she had unknowingly done. Had she not captured Martin's heart for all time he would have done the honourable thing on learning of Ellen's pregnancy. He would have married her, made her son legitimate, and, from his initial pity for her, his affection, love could have grown. Adam had to be very big in spirit indeed to be able to defend her lies, wild imaginings and spite.

'Hungry?' He had finished placing the food on the cloth and he patted the soft carpet beside him. 'I never could resist a picnic—even indoors. So humour me?'

Whether they ate at a table, with style and formality, or from paper bags was immaterial to her. This was probably the last meal they would ever share. So she sat beside him, cross-legged on the floor, and tried to forget all that painful regret, the cold knowledge that by the time this day ended she would have walked out of his life.

And she succeeded, because she was determined she would, and his air of having relaxed completely helped. So did the wine, the food they ate with their fingers, the crackle of the logs on the hearth—so much so that when the last crumb was eaten, the last drop of wine consumed, and he leant back against the base of one of the armchairs and pulled her with him, she didn't object.

She was too comfortable, too relaxed and drowsy to pull herself to her feet and tell him it was time they left, and when he cupped the side of her face with a gentle hand and asked, 'Would you like to see over the rest of the house?' she murmured,

'Later,' not wanting to move, not able to, closing her mind to danger.

And his thumb began to stroke the slanting line of her cheekbones, his fingertips following, gently, idly almost, caressing the corner of her mouth, the angle of her jaw, sliding across soft skin, down the length of her neck as if he were a blind man, seeking to identify her by touch. And when he began to tug at her braid, releasing her hair, running his hands through the glorious, spilling riot of tawny silk, she instinctively turned her face, burrowing into him, her lips pressed against the pulse-point at the base of his warm, satiny throat. She tasted his skin, the musky maleness of him, and slid lower, lower, to where the warm olive-toned satin was roughened by crisp dark hair.

She heard the harsh intake of his breath, felt the heavy beat of her heart between them as sensation, as swift as it was sure, blotted out the last of her thought processes.

She forgot everything in a passionate need to touch and be touched, aching for the fulfilment only he could give her, and could only moan incoherently when she discovered that they were lying fully on the hearthrug, had slid away from the support of the chair without her realising it.

He was propped up on one elbow, his big body half covering hers, and the slitted green eyes as they studied her flushed face were sensuality incarnate. And she was drowning; she knew she was, drowning in heat and need and glorious fever. Her mouth opened to accept his as his dark head dipped, and it was possession, hunger, his shafting tongue a statement of intent.

Following the impulsive dictates of her body, she writhed against him, arching in exquisite near-agony as his hand slid beneath the hem of her sweater and found her engorged breasts, playing with them until she thought she would die of the rioting torment. And she clung to his mouth, demanding, pleading, and bit back a sob of frustration as, idly teasing each hard, aroused nipple in turn, he drew his mouth from hers, lifted his head, his eyes hard, his mouth harder.

And in that breathless, cold moment of time she remembered. Yet, even though she knew why he was doing this, rousing her weak body until she was on the point of going down on her knees, pleading with him for ecstasy he promised yet never delivered, she couldn't quite believe it was happening all over again, that she had stupidly allowed him to do this to her.

Any moment now he would walk away, slap her down and walk away, that humiliating contempt in his eyes. And she didn't know why.

Not knowing why was even worse than the shame of having allowed him to torment her yet again, the agony of unfulfilled need, the bitter ache of wanting.

A sob filled her throat and almost broke, and her voice was a straining thread of sound as she shifted away from him and demanded, 'Why are you doing this? You don't want me!'

There followed a slow, silent beat of time until, unforgivably, his mouth curved in that indolent, shattering smile, his eyes glinting down into hers, his unforgettably unique voice a sensual caress as he murmured, 'Don't I? That's news to me, sweetheart. Like me to prove you wrong?'

CHAPTER TEN

'NO!' SELINA gasped raggedly, twisting away, trying to scramble to her feet. But Adam rolled over, his strong arms making her captive as he pulled her back, the top half of his body pinning her down.

'But I say yes!' he said tauntingly, glinting down into her wild golden eyes. 'You can't make statements like that and expect them to go unchallenged.'

Naked desire was staining the hard lines of his cheekbones, the green eyes brooding darkly with passion, and she gave a choked half-sob, her hands pushing against the impervious wall of his chest. A log fell into the heart of the fire, the light of the brightly flaring flames stroking the carved, beautiful lines of his face.

'How can you say I don't want you?' His mouth came closer, a tormenting breath of space above hers, and she dragged in a tortured gasp of air and reminded him, and herself, because she was in mortal danger of forgetting all over again, 'You walk away. You always walk away.'

'Ah.' The gleam of understanding was a pin-point of light in the drowning green depths of his eyes. It was the last thing she saw as he closed each eyelid with a kiss. And his mouth drifted down to lie against hers as he whispered, 'It wasn't easy, sweetheart. It took all my self-control to step back when all I wanted to do was take what you were offering.'

'Oooh!' A tiny spurt of indignation struggled to find expression, but was slaughtered by the voluptuous sensation of the silken heat of his lips as they moved so tantalisingly against hers, and she moaned softly, desire

163

for him a chemical reaction that was turning her body to liquid fire.

The tip of his tongue explored a corner of her mouth then roved across her languorously parted lips to find the other, and the slow beat of his own need was there in the soft darkness of his voice as he murmured, 'You had to grow to like me a little before we made love together. I needed that. Selfish, hmm?' His tongue delved deeper, explored the helplessly willing moistness of her mouth and then withdrew, his teeth nipping at her lower lip, his tongue lapping the tiny damage as he told her, 'Until today, I think, all you've done is resent me, distrust me. I think it's different now.'

Selina's heart swelled and ached within her; just how different he didn't know. The aftermath of the shocking impact of sudden realisation filled her with sadness. She loved him.

How long had she been resisting that self-defeating knowledge? For how long had she stubbornly hidden it from herself?

A burning tear emerged saltily from beneath her closed eyelids and his lingering tongue lapped it away. And the intimacy, the closeness, the utter hopelessness of that one triste moment defeated her, the pain in her heart almost more than she could bear.

'Don't,' he commanded throatily. 'Everything's going to be fine now. Believe me.'

Believe him? How could she, when she knew better? Falling in love with him had made everything so disastrously wrong. Yet how could she explain that, without giving herself away? The last thing he wanted to hear was some maudlin female bleating away about love! Love, for him, was a silly illusion, one he wanted no part of.

She pushed feebly at his shoulders; the tense musculature was riven by small tremors of need, and the feeble attempt to escape was transformed to a lusty, impatient tug because her own consuming desire for him overrode everything else. Common sense, caution, self-preservation became non-existent. This was all she would ever have of him; this was to be the making of a memory she would have to live on for the rest of her life.

But he denied the impetuous demands of her clinging hands, capturing them, uncurling each palm to place a kiss in the centre of them before sitting back on his heels, sliding his hands beneath her body and pulling her across his knees, cradling her head to kiss her so thoroughly that she had no time to think of anything other than this timeless, drugging sensation.

But it wasn't enough, not nearly enough, the savage glitter of his eyes as she tangled her fingers in his hair, the insistent throbbing that was shaking her whole body, taking over; all told her that it was not enough, not for either of them.

And if it had just been this, this need, this wanting, just this for both of them, then she would have gone along with his devious, inexplicable charade and allowed him to think he was successfully blackmailing her into marriage. A marriage filled with the glorious savagery of mutual desire, respect and liking, well, that could have been enough. But loving him...

One last attempt to salvage her principles, her self-respect had her voice sounding strangled as she forced out the statement, 'You would never have carried out those threats against Martin. Even if I'd refused to even think of marrying you, you couldn't have hurt him.' And that was as far as she could get along the road to telling him that after today she would never see him again, because he was slowly undressing her, taking time between kissing the nakedness he uncovered to mutter thickly,

'I wondered how long it would take you to cotton on.' His mouth found and relished the turgid tip of one breast, suckling there until she gasped and writhed with the exquisite pain-pleasure, needing no second invitation when he begged hoarsely, 'Touch me! Ah, please, sweetheart, touch me!'

Something between a sob and a groan forced itself from the depths of her being as she helped him undress, her hands shaking, all but useless as they tangled with the thickly crisp body hair above the zip of his dark brown cords while she arched her neck to smother the quivering muscles of his magnificent, bared chest with avid, moist kisses until his hands clenched on her naked shoulders in a spasm of need, recalling her to the task in hand.

And when, between them, they'd shakily dealt with his nether garments and he was as unashamedly naked as she, she closed her hands around his gloriously, savagely aroused manhood and closed her eyes as pure, blissful ecstasy rocked her to the very depths of her soul. And she was drowning in it, drowning on expiring little gasps, drawn deeper and deeper into the pounding maelstrom of her desire for him, her love for him as he lowered her, covering her feverish body with his, parting her thighs...

There was a brief moment when her tightness held them both still for an infinitesimal flicker of time, and then he was driving within her, each stroke, each dizzying plunge and slow withdrawal transporting her higher and higher, far beyond space and time and reality, deep into the infinity of the final, ultimate, exquisite intimacy...

*   *   *

Selina was encompassed by a sensuous sensation of faintly throbbing fulfilment, dreamy, entirely and utterly pleasant. She knew she had to think, think hard and fast. But now wasn't the time. Not while she was still cocooned in the sheer wonder, the exhilaration, the glorious memory of the repeated and blissful, blissful ecstasy of Adam's lovemaking.

The dashboard clock showed a little after midnight and the thrumming of the tyres on the road surface was hypnotic, increasing her dreamy drowsiness, and she stifled an aching yawn.

They had left the cottage barely an hour ago, and she was still aware of the wrench, the feeling that she had left something precious behind, the knowledge that she would never find it again, that what they had finally closed the door on was lost and gone forever.

But she wasn't going to think about that now. She really couldn't bear to, and she was thankful that Adam, like she, didn't seem to need the triviality of small talk but preferred to stay with his own thoughts.

Briefly, she wondered what they were, what he was thinking. And decided that, on the whole, she would rather not know.

Sighing, she allowed herself the one luxury of a sideways glance in his direction. The lights of the dashboard gently illuminated his chiselled profile, and she saw, with a melting pang of love, that the harshness of the memorably bold outline was totally obviated by the kiss-softened sensuality of his beautiful mouth.

Selina sighed again, curled deeper into the comfortable leather seat, and slept.

She came awake, her arms wound tightly around his neck, her face buried in the soft wool of his shirt, her nostrils filled with the tantalising, sheer male scent of him. Briefly disorientated, her grip tightened to a stranglehold and his steps faltered, but only for a moment, before the huskiness of his rough velvet voice sent unstoppable shivers down her spine.

'I thought you'd never wake.'

He was carrying her up the stairs, back at his house in town. Her eyes focused, recognising the surroundings, and her poor heart fluttered and almost stood still as he pushed the door to his bedroom open with his foot and carried her over to his bed.

Setting her on the coverlet as if she were some rare object, infinitely precious and highly fragile, he looked down at her with bedroom eyes and offered, 'Shall I undress you now, or after I've fetched the champagne?'

Something spiteful gnawed at the aching edges of her heart and she repeated stupidly, through the pain of it, 'Champagne?'

'To celebrate.' One of his hands gently pushed the tousled hair back from her ashen face, and the warmth of his smile was like spring sunlight after winter.

But it didn't warm her, didn't touch her. She mustn't let it. And she didn't, not even when he explained huskily, 'I've had it on ice ever since I met you, waiting for this moment.'

The moment when he knew he'd won, when he recognised her acceptance of the kind of marriage he had in mind? She didn't know. There were still so many things she didn't know. But she wasn't asking. The questions would remain unspoken, unanswered for all eternity. Did his reasons for picking on her, using blackmailing threats he had never had any intention of carrying out, really matter?

No, of course they didn't, she answered herself. How could they matter when the only thing that counted now was untangling herself from a relationship that threatened to ruin the rest of her life, break her completely?

She endured one last caress of his hands, endured that final tender pain, and watched with nearly blind eyes as he walked out of the door, leaving her with the lazy injunction to stay right where she was.

And then she had to move. She had to force herself to her feet, her legs shamefully unsteady. She couldn't possibly spend the rest of her life with him, knowing he would never love her, knowing he'd married her because they were good in bed together and he wanted a mother for his children.

If she did, her love would turn to anguish, to bitterness. She would start to hate him for the hold he had over her, hate herself for being so weak, despise herself for grabbing the fool's gold of his lust instead of waiting for the pure gold of love.

Why, oh, why had she ever been so stupid? If she hadn't learned to love him, she could have married him on his terms because they would have been her terms, too. A good sexual relationship, mutual liking and respect, children. An equal partnership, clear-cut and simple. Many an excellent marriage had been based on far less.

But falling in love with him had made it unequal, the scales all weighted on his side. She couldn't short-change herself to that extent; pride and what was left of her self-respect, her instinctive need for self-preservation, wouldn't let her.

It wouldn't be long before he returned with that champagne and found her missing, she told herself, trying to organise her frantic movements into some semblance of order as she threw things haphazardly into her suitcase back in her own room.

And it wasn't long, not nearly long enough, she thought as she quailed inwardly beneath the cool questioning of his eyes as he stepped through the door, recognising the chaos, the reason for it.

'Going somewhere?' The sensuous mouth displayed the tight cruelty of sarcasm, and she gave him back a wild look of desperation, knowing what she was going to have to say if she was to have any hope at all of him letting her go.

It wouldn't be easy, she thought, her mind in turmoil, her fingers practically shredding the flimsy pieces of underwear grabbed out of one of the drawers. It would be the most difficult, distasteful thing she'd ever been called on to do.

'How on earth did you guess?' She could match his sarcasm any day of the week, she told herself staunchly, and turned away from him, tossing the mangled briefs and bras into the case. And he said, as if even now he couldn't believe it,

'Why?' He took a sharp intake of breath. 'Selina— what the hell's going on here? What's wrong? Look at me, dammit, and tell me what's wrong!'

She didn't; of course she didn't. She kept her back firmly turned on him, afraid to look at him in case it all came spilling out. All of it—the way she loved him, the way parting from him would be like tearing away half of her soul, the fear she had that over the years her love would turn to hate because he would make her sexually dependent on him and, because there was nothing more for him, she would despise herself, hate him.

And still she couldn't bring herself to say the words that would send him away. Trying to disguise the weak way her legs were trembling, she knelt down in front of the bottom drawer in the dressing-chest and dragged out an armful of sweaters, her heart pounding so heavily that she didn't hear his swift, soft-footed approach until two inescapable hands fastened round her upper arms, dragging her to her feet and swinging her round to face him.

'Tell me, dammit!' he bit out through his teeth. 'Why should you walk out on me? Now, of all times!'

Why indeed? she thought drearily, and said aloud, 'Don't ask. You might not like the answer.' He was too close, too male, much too dear to her, his hands slowly relaxing their relentless grip on her arms, gradually beginning to move in tiny, soothing circles, and she couldn't bear it, couldn't bear to think of what she was losing, throwing away, yet couldn't bear to think of the sterile alternative either.

With an effort of will which had her skin pulled back against her facial bones, making her look hard, she instructed tightly, 'Get your hands off me. Don't touch me,' and saw the flicker of derision in his eyes before she looked quickly away, her heart beating sickeningly as he continued that undermining, hypnotic caress. His voice was a tone darker than midnight as he reminded her silkily, 'You weren't saying that a few hours ago.'

If she listened to that compelling voice for one moment longer, to the betraying siren song that coursed wildly through her blood whenever he was near, she would surrender, agree to anything he wanted, and regret it to the end of her life.

Selina ground her teeth together in a desperate effort for control, and, her head lifted proudly, her long golden eyes defying his, took the only escape route open to her, telling him crudely, 'Too true. But I hadn't had you then, had I? I wanted you, but you knew that, of course. And now I've had you. End of story.'

She saw his face tighten, the bones sharply prominent behind the skin, but he still looked as if he couldn't believe what he was hearing. So she tacked on tonelessly, just for good measure, 'You didn't think I'd marry you, did you? Nothing you could threaten me with could make me walk up the aisle with a man I didn't love, who didn't love me.'

She thought he might kill her then, and didn't much care if he did, but after taut seconds, when unleashed violence made the still air scream with turbulence, he thrust her aside with a grossly unflattering epithet which left her in no doubt at all as to the way he viewed her.

She closed her eyes to hide the pain and when she had the strength to force them open again she saw through a shimmer of scalding tears that she was alone.

And if he walked back in right now she would fling herself into his arms and sob out the truth. All of it. And let the future look after itself, she confessed, ragged with the pain of what she'd done, all the fight drained out of her.

But he didn't come back.

And she knew he never would.

'Of course you can come,' Vanessa broke smoothly into Selina's muddled excuses. 'It isn't as if it's a spur-of-the-moment thing; you've got a whole ten days to re-arrange your social schedule. It isn't as if Dominic gets engaged every day of the week. And you'll like Tanya. She's a lovely girl off the catwalk, nothing like the usual run of harpies he's been mixing with. Of course, all her people are in Tasmania; her mother was widowed early in life and moved out there—to be with relatives, I believe—but has married since, very well, too, from what I can gather. There's certainly no lack of money.'

Her aunt burbled on and Selina closed her eyes and began to wish she hadn't answered the phone, hadn't rushed to pick it up, her heart thrumming because it might—it just conceivably might—be Adam.

It never was, of course. She'd been at the flat for two whole months, ever since she'd walked out of his house that night. And he must know she was here. He owned the place. She thought he might have come, or phoned, if only to tell her in no uncertain terms to get out.

One day she was going to have to find a place of her own, some place he didn't own. But all her energies had been put into her work, leaving little spare for anything else. And the very thought of mixing with the usual crowd at one of her aunt's parties made her feel very tired indeed.

'What about Martin?' she cut into Vanessa's monologue, catching something about, 'Dig out your best finery, it's going to be quite a thrash,' wondering how her uncle would weather it. He'd made excellent progress, but one of Vanessa's parties was enough to make the strongest man quail, let alone one so recently recovering from a heart attack. But her aunt assured her loftily,

'I do know what I'm doing. After helping Dom, Tanya and myself to greet our guests, having a teeny drink, he will retire gracefully to his room to play chess with Dr Hill.'

So that was that taken care of and, thankfully, Vanessa ran out of steam soon afterwards and Selina put down the phone and turned the sound back up on the television set.

Trying to avoid Dom's engagement party had been instinctive. She had avoided all social contacts since the break with Adam, spending all her spare time here at the flat, either with work brought home from the office or staring with uncomprehending, sad, blank eyes at the television screen.

She switched it off.

She had to stop behaving so stupidly. Whenever she thought of the way she had got Adam to back off she felt degraded, her insides curling with distaste. But it had been necessary. And, she reminded herself tartly, it was all in the past. Over. He would never want to set eyes on her again, and she couldn't blame him. He would never come here to the flat while she was in residence; he probably loathed the very thought of her.

And seeing him again was the last thing she wanted, wasn't it? Nothing had changed; he would never love her, he wouldn't let himself. Seeing him again would bring her nothing but grief. So tomorrow she would begin flat-hunting in earnest.

There was no way she could go back to live at the Hall. Until the debt was repaid, Adam owned that, too. Or, at least, his bank did, which amounted to the same thing. Besides, she really did need to be on her own, because she seemed to have grown out of her surrogate family since meeting Adam.

Not that she loved them any the less, of course, and her feeling of having grown away from them was hard to explain. She still enjoyed visiting at the weekends, grateful because after an initial look of surprise no one, except Martin, had said a word about the breaking-off of her so-called engagement to Adam Tudor. And Martin had merely said, 'I don't know what happened, and won't ask. But, take it from me, Adam won't let go so easily.'

Little did Martin know! Getting her back was the very last thing Adam would want. She had said that terrible thing to make sure of just that.

Sighing, she went through to the kitchen to prepare her evening meal, decided she didn't fancy anything and made do with a cup of coffee. She drank it standing up at the kitchen counter and then went to bed and lay in the darkness, telling herself that she had the rest of her life to get on with and, in the circumstances, she should be supremely thankful that Adam Tudor would have no part in it.

She almost convinced herself, too, and spent the following week flat-hunting. Those she liked she couldn't afford and those she could afford were horrid. But it was early days, she assured herself, and something fantastic might turn up next week. Besides, she was going to have to find something to wear for Dom's party. She had lost so much weight recently that nothing she owned fitted properly.

Making herself take an interest, she bought an outrageously daring cocktail dress and splurged on a whole new range of make-up, then spent the rest of the day regretting it because she'd need every spare penny she had to use as a deposit when she eventually found a flat she liked.

A sudden spate of work, intricate telephone calls to suppliers on the Continent, meant she had to go in to the office on the Saturday of the party, and she was late setting out for the Hall and only had time to greet Tanya briefly before heading for her old bedroom to change.

Dom seemed far more sober, she mused as she took a quick shower. The arrogant, pugnacious quality of old had disappeared, and he'd seemed touchingly protective of his brand new fiancée, already dressed in her finery— a floor-length blue silk sheath that suited her slender blonde beauty to perfection.

Falling in love, coupled with the dressing-down he must have had from his father and Adam, and the spectre of the law courts, might be the making of him. She hoped so.

Although her own conversation with Tanya had been necessarily short, she'd picked up enough vibes to tell her why Vanessa had deemed this one young woman a suitable match for her own precious son. Despite her exquisite beauty, the girl seemed shy, anxious to please, and obviously adored the ground Dominic walked on. And of course she came from a wealthy background, which would help, Selina thought cynically as she smoothed body oil into her skin.

The anguish of parting from the one man she could ever love had wreaked havoc with her looks, she decided drearily as she blow-dried her tawny mane of hair. But the new conditioner she'd used had given it back some of its former gloss and bounce—although doing precious little to make it more manageable.

The new make-up and dress helped, too, of course, although, on sober consideration, the short-skirted, blouse-topped gold tissue dress, with its plunging neckline back and front, was perhaps much too outrageously sexy.

Dragging the few things she'd left behind here from their hangers, she could come up with nothing remotely suitable that might fit her new, slenderised frame, and gave the exercise up as a bad job.

There was no time to change now, anyway, even if she could have found something partyish to fit. She'd heard the first of the guests arrive as she'd scurried upstairs to get ready, and if she spent any longer in her room her aunt would accuse her of wanting to steal the limelight, or sulking.

She knew the main reception-rooms had been turned into buffets and bars, complete with comfortable groups of armchairs and tables, with linen-covered trestles set out with the delicious finger-food Meg had probably spent all week preparing. And the huge hall had been cleared for dancing, she noted, as she walked slowly down the main staircase.

The music was loud and already a few couples were dancing, but the night was very young yet and more were content to watch, concentrating on the food on their plates, talking. Everything would get far more animated as the evening wore on, she knew, and wondered how she would get through it—then knew she wouldn't get through it at all when she felt the piercing power of someone's scrutiny and the blood turned to ice in her veins as she met Adam's bleak green stare.

He was standing near the great fireplace where the woodburner was emitting a gentle heat. He looked so devastating in formal evening gear that her stupid heart turned over inside her.

Shocked, almost mesmerised, she saw him turn to his companion, a striking brunette who seemed to have been poured into the scarlet silk she was wearing. He said something, something with a smile, but his face was like stone as he turned back again and began to stride across to the staircase.

She had to make it back to her room, get away from the nightmare of seeing him again. She was already halfway down the staircase now and she turned, her heart knocking violently against her breastbone. But the tightness of her short skirt, the ridiculously high heels she always favoured, made it impossible to hurry, to make much progress at all. And sheer, blind panic didn't help, and made her gasp wildly as she sensed him closing in behind her, her heart beating in her throat now, choking her!

And the pressure of his hand on her elbow as he reached her side, the searing sensation of skin on skin, made her bones collapse, her legs giving way beneath her, his hand supporting her the only reason she was able to stay upright.

'Look pleased to see me,' he commanded in a harsh undertone as she stared up at him with frantic eyes. 'And walk, woman, walk.' He was smiling down at her, but it was empty, a feral smile of intense contempt. His hand hauled on her elbow, edging her upwards. 'Martin told half the world, it seems, about our engagement. If you make the sort of scene I can sense you're brewing, we'll be the subject of malicious gossip into the foreseeable future.'

'Go away!' she spat out of the corner of her mouth. Seeing him again, having him touch her, was purgatory. She loved him so much, wanted him so badly. His being here had filled all that emptiness she'd been trying to cope with, with a pain the like of which she had never dreamed possible.

'Didn't you listen to what I said? Or are you too damn selfish to care?' He was still wearing that empty smile for the benefit of anyone who might be watching, but his words were laced with bitter disgust and she spat back at him,

'The engagement's broken, for what it was ever worth!'

'Tell me something I don't know.' He bared his teeth, the unresistable pressure of his hand pushing her onwards, tottering on her four-inch heels. 'But others don't, as yet. And for Martin's sake it has to be done with some kind of dignity. Fighting me on a staircase in full view of a hundred people isn't the way to achieve it.'

There was a raucous cheer from the younger, raunchier guests below as they reached the head of the stairs, a cheer that left Selina in no doubt that everyone believed he couldn't wait to get her alone. Her face ran scarlet with mortification and Adam said nastily, 'You asked for that. If you dress like a walking bedroom invitation, don't be surprised when you get that kind of reaction. Who were you hoping to have "had" by tomorrow morning? Don't tell me. I'm really not interested.'

For a moment she was too stunned by what he had said to make any protest, merely staring at him, her mouth open in shocked outrage. They had veered off into the corridor that led to the wing of the house that had been her own domain since she'd come here as an orphaned ten-year-old, and he stopped, bending down and removing her shoes. And for a moment something about his attitude, the curve of those strong hands, told her he was about to touch her ankles, run his hands over her silk-clad calves, her thighs. She went dizzy, and felt drugged, anticipation making her tremble, her mouth go dry.

But he merely straightened, holding her shoes in one hand and urging her forwards with the other, informing her coldly, 'Perhaps we'll make slightly better progress now.'

Sheer, stupid disappointment made her feel sick. But she hadn't really wanted him to touch her, certainly not, she assured herself firmly. There was no future for them, never had been, never would be. And although the unforgivable remark about the way she was dressed still hurt unbearably it was better to leave him to think what he liked.

'Then what does interest you?' she asked coldly, not willing to let him get away entirely with that snide remark, wishing she could tug her skirt even higher than it was so that she could keep up with his brisk pace without having to mince along like a ruptured duck. And, reaching the door of her bedroom, he ushered her in, telling her,

'Getting our stories straight. Finding a reasonable excuse for ending our relationship, and sticking to it. Unfortunately——' he walked into the room '—Martin seems to be of the opinion that it's only a matter of time before we come to our senses—his words, not mine—and patch things up. He can be remarkably stubborn when he thinks he knows best. Which is why he has so far refused to tell anyone, apart from Vanessa—in strictest confidence—that the forthcoming wedding is off. We have to decide what to tell him to convince him it's not. And I don't think the real reasons will make him a happy man, do you?'

He had been pacing the carpet and now he turned, his brows coming down in a frowning black bar as he instructed tersely, 'For pity's sake, woman, come in and shut the door. And you needn't worry, I'm not going to touch you. No matter how inviting the package, I've gone off what's inside.'

'Lucky for you!' she sniped back, hating him for that insult, not bothering to hide it. 'Because you're not getting any! In any case——' she forced herself forward, not bothering to close the door because he wouldn't be staying '—when Vanessa discovers you're here, complete with someone who looks as if the dress she's wearing has been painted on, she'll throw you out. How did you get over the doorstep, anyway? Disguise yourself as a waiter? Or did you pretend to be the boy who carries out the trash?'

She, she discovered, could be as nasty as he. And if she dare not let her love for him flower and flourish she could damn well hate him! But, apart from an unnerving gleam in those magnificent green eyes, he seemed to ignore the insults, telling her more levelly, 'Vanessa knows I'm here. She sent me the invitation. Martin, apparently, has told her the truth—about Ellen, what she was really like, about seeing me over the years. There are no more secrets between them now, thank God. And Vanessa has responded by admitting how wrong she's been, forcing Martin and myself apart—as she thought. Married couples shouldn't have secrets. And as I am now openly welcomed into Vanessa's charmed family circle,' he informed her drily, 'we two have to get our act together. We can't be seen to be flying at each other's throat every time we meet.'

'I don't want us to meet,' she responded dully, pattering on her stockinged feet to the armchair beneath the window. She was glad that Martin and Vanessa had straightened things out, that her aunt had been big enough to admit her past mistakes, that Adam wouldn't be regarded as the skeleton in the cupboard. He didn't deserve that. But she couldn't bear to meet up with Adam, over the years, at the family celebrations Vanessa always made such a thing of.

So where did that leave her?

Perched on the edge of the big chair, she plucked miserably at the gold fabric of her skirt and heard him say darkly, 'Why not? Because you're ashamed of yourself? Of what you did, what you said? You know——' he had closed the door and was moving over the floor towards her '—I don't think you're the promiscuous tramp you made yourself out to be. I was too damned hurt, too disgusted to work it out for a while. But when we made love—well——' He was standing over her now, his powerful body threatening. 'Not to put too fine a point on it, if you weren't a virgin it had been a long, long time since you had slept with a man.'

Selina drew in a painful breath, wishing she had the physical strength to throw him out of the room. His questions, his statement were all too near the bone for her liking. And when she refused to comment he went on harshly, 'You tried to make me believe that you were the sort who would sleep with any man who took your fancy, and then walk away and look for another. When I'd calmed down enough to think straight, I knew you'd been lying. I can only deduce you deliberately set out to wound me as deeply as you knew how. I don't know why. I don't think I really want to. But you needn't have used lies to end our relationship. The truth, whatever it was, would have sufficed. Now——' He swung the stool from in front of her dressing-table and planted it in front of where she sat, dropping down on it, dipping his head so that his eyes were on a level with hers. 'What we have to decide on is a reason for our break-up, one that's fit for public consumption.'

Anger, pain and humiliation made a distasteful cocktail of emotions, and Selina wasn't going to swallow it. He could concoct whatever story he liked, and she'd go along with it, but he couldn't get away with calling her a liar!

And she wasn't going to sit here, like a thunder-struck mouse, and take all the insults he felt like dishing out.

Adrenalin pushed her to her feet, made her drag her fingers through her hair, made her brush aside the hands that would have pushed her back in her seat.

'Don't be so bloody pompous!' she yelped at him, her eyes narrowed to spitting golden slits, all the regrets, the heartache of losing him translating to blinding, furious loss of all that careful control. 'You talk about lying as if I invented the pastime! Lying to end the relationship—my aunt Fanny! It was you and your whoppers that started it! Deny that, if you can, Mr Holier-Than-Thou!' She was well into her stride now, in more ways than one. She didn't notice when the tight gold fabric split along the seam, giving her the freedom to stalk around the room, didn't notice his eyes narrow, the bright intelligence of the clever mind showing through in sharp emerald glints.

'It's all right for you to come along, overflowing with lies about blackmail, what you'd do if I refused to marry you. Me—why me? Someone you'd never met before in your life! "Marry me, or I'll make a holocaust", or words to that effect! And lies—all of it lies!'

She twisted on her heels to face him, her hands on her slender hips. He had taken the chair she had been using. But why bother about that? He had already taken everything else from her. He was leaning back, his head tilted slightly to one side, one knee crossed negligently over the other. As if he were watching a bloody pantomime, she thought, infuriated all over again.

'So don't come the Holy Joe with me——' She thrust her face close to his, her eyes wild and stormy. 'I only lied to defend myself. You lied because it gave you a perverted pleasure to frighten me silly, to get me to fall in love with you and go to bed with you. The only true words you ever said was when you told me you couldn't love, didn't want to love anyone, thought it was all an illusion!'

Suddenly, all the colour drained from her face; she felt it go, felt the shaking begin inside her as, too late, far too late, she realised what she'd said. She'd admitted to loving him. Had he taken it in?

The shaking got worse. She couldn't look at him, and sagged down on to the stool at his feet, because it was either that or the floor, and buried her face in her hands. Of course he had taken it in. He wasn't a fool. And there was nothing to be done about it now, except weather his scorn, his pity, perhaps. And when his hands covered hers, drawing them away from her face, she didn't resist, and was covered in shame when she saw the way her split skirt was tangled up somewhere at the very top of her thighs.

She tried to do something about it, but he held on to her hands, standing up and drawing her with him as he commanded, 'Say that again. Say you love me.'

Selina hung her head, tangled hair hiding her face. She wouldn't. She couldn't. Once had been one time too many; she wasn't going to be forced into compounding her own humiliation.

'Will it help if I tell you that you were right—that yes, I did lie, and go on lying until you'd formed your own judgements, reached the right conclusions? But that I was telling the truth, as I saw it, when I said I'd never fall in love, looked on the emotion as a fable, an illusion.' He brushed the riot of hair back from her face and cupped her chin, forcing the hypnotic strength of his gaze on her, his lips only inches away from the quivering, miserable pout of her mouth.

He'd gone and admitted his inability to love again! Her lower lip trembled alarmingly and his gaze dropped, drawn to the give-away sign, and his lips dropped, too, soothing lips, covering hers, whispering against hers, 'I kept my own self-delusion to the bitter end. Right up to when you walked out on me. I knew I wanted you as I've never wanted any other woman. And not only in my bed, but in my life, every part of it. But I didn't know I loved you until you walked out.' He drew her suddenly compliant body into his arms, cradling her bright head against the black fabric that covered his chest. 'I didn't know what was worse—the pain of loving you and losing you, or the pain of what you had said.'

'You mean that?' Slowly, her head came up. She'd been crying, and hadn't realised it. All over his jacket, too. She made an ineffectual effort to wipe away the dampness but his hand captured hers, carrying it up to his mouth, kissing each fingertip.

'More than I've ever meant anything before.'

'Then—then what were you doing with that woman?' And, at his blank expression, 'The one who'd been poured into a red silk dress.'

'Talking. Passing time until you put in an appearance.' He grinned unashamedly. 'Poured in her dress, hmm? Pity I was too preoccupied to notice it. I believe she was one of Tanya's model friends.' And then he kissed her, taking her breath away, making her dizzy, so that she could only stare at him bemusedly when he dragged his mouth from hers and stated, 'The wedding's on again.'

It took a moment or two before she was able to answer. He'd been very aroused when he'd been kissing her. Very. She shook her head to clear it, her eyes widening as she felt his fingers deal with the back zip of her dress. And she said shakily, very aroused herself now and revelling in it, 'Of course. I would have married you anyway, before I knew I loved you—at least,' she amended honestly, 'I think I would. The idea was tempting because you were the most fanciable man I'd ever met. Then, when I'd worked out that no way would you harm Martin, or any one of his family, and found myself in love with you, I couldn't marry you. You'd told me you didn't believe in love.'

She didn't know if she was making much sense, because he'd removed her dress entirely, stripping the gold tissue away from her body and tossing it over the foot of the bed. Next thing, he'd be tearing off her scanty underwear. Her lips parted in lush invitation, her breasts pushing unashamedly against the delicate lacy covering. But he must have understood what she'd been trying to say because he replied, almost sombrely, 'I understand that now,' and walked over to her wardrobe, flicking through the remaining contents and tossing an old pair of jeans and a raincoat that had seen better days in her direction.

She caught them, holding them to her, her eyes widening in disbelief as he rummaged through a drawer and came up with a sweater. She caught that, too, and managed breathily, 'What are you doing?'

She had been so certain he was about to make love to her, and her disappointment was shameful, but unmistakable, but her heart flipped inside her with joy as he told her, 'Getting you dressed. You can't make the journey to the cottage in that bit of nonsense. We'll make our get-away down the back staircase and phone when we get there, just to let them know where we are.'

'We're going to the Cotswolds!'

It wasn't a question, it was a burble of joy. She'd go to the North Pole with him if he told her to. And he said, helping her push her legs into the old worn jeans, 'And that's where we're staying until the day before our wedding. I do not, and I repeat not intend letting you out of my sight again.'

And that was fine by her, just fine. But as her head emerged from the neck of her sweater and he smoothed back her tangled mane of hair she asked, 'Why did you threaten me with blackmail? Couldn't you have courted me like a normal guy?' and saw embarrassment darken his eyes.

'Darn it, woman. You ask the most awkward questions!' But he wasn't the type to suffer embarrassment for long, she noted as that charismatic grin beaconed out. 'They say there's no fool like a man in love,' he excused as he helped her into the raincoat and fastened the buttons up the front. 'And, looking back, I'm prepared to believe I fell in love with you as soon as I saw you.' He threaded the belt through the buckle and tightened it. 'You've lost weight. We're going to have to do something about that.'

'So?' She prodded his apparently failing memory.

'So——' He dragged her into his arms. 'So I felt I knew you before I met you. I'd seen photographs of you, too; Martin was always so proud of you. And I'd spoken to you, on the phone, remember? You had the sexiest voice.'

She said, 'Snap!' huskily, but he couldn't have heard because he was telling her,

'And when I actually saw you in the flesh I thought, This is the woman I want for my wife. The mother of my children, a lifelong partner. And wondered how long it would take you to come round to my way of thinking. And you treated me as if I were a reject from the Mafia, and I knew Vanessa must have been getting at you and knew it would take forever and a day to get you to lose that haughty look and begin to see me as a man instead of something despicable.'

She moved closer to him, pressing her body against his, winding her arms around his neck, her fingers tangling in the short black hair, finding the hardness of bone beneath. She had been a bitch to him, she remembered with a pang of love so intense that it took her breath away, and she couldn't blame him for his consequent action, especially when he confessed, 'I acted so much out of character, blackmailing you that way, that I must have been in love with you, right from the start. Nothing else can explain the rage I felt, the feeling that as I held all the cards I'd use them, and damn the consequences. I told myself that, to begin with, it was a way of cutting you down to size, forcing you into my company. It would only be a matter of time before you worked things out for yourself and realised it was all a bluff. And then we could get to know each other on level terms. If I hadn't done it, you wouldn't have given me the time of day, let alone come to live with me, and——'

She stopped his words with her lips and when they pulled breathlessly apart she said jerkily, 'We could stay here tonight. If we lock the door and——'

But he shook his head, his eyes dancing.

'The idea's tempting, believe me, sweetheart.' Then he rearranged all the clothing that had somehow come adrift between them. 'But you're my woman and I'm having you on my own home ground. Now. Always. Move.'

And later, how much later she was too happy to question, she snuggled more deeply into his arms in the wide double bed in the heart of the hidden valley, the tip of her tongue tasting the salt of his skin as she asked him huskily, 'Do you think they're wondering where we are? We forgot to phone.'

'I expect they'll guess.' Seducing hands cupped her buttocks and roved around the feminine flare of her hips. 'I was preoccupied. And I expect we're going to forget to do a lot of things, don't you?' His hands slid round to her bottom again, pressing her tightly against the hardness of him. 'Do you think you might like to have me again?'

And she bit back a giggle at that teasing reminder and answered both questions in one dreamy breath.

'I shouldn't be surprised if we forgot our names, and oh, yes, please!'

**This June, Harlequin invites
you to a wedding of**

Promised Brides

Celebrate the joy and romance of weddings past with
PROMISED BRIDES—a collection of original historical short
stories, written by three best-selling historical authors:

> *The Wedding of the Century*—MARY JO PUTNEY
> *Jesse's Wife*—KRISTIN JAMES
> *The Handfast*—JULIE TETEL

Three unforgettable heroines, three award-winning authors!
PROMISED BRIDES is available in June wherever Harlequin
Books are sold.

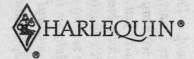

HARLEQUIN®

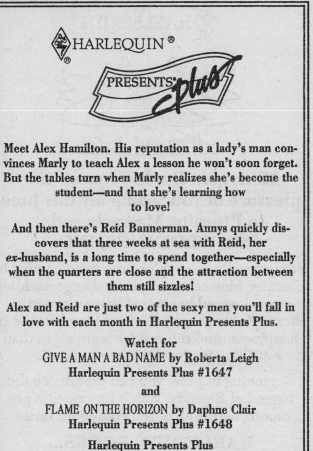

Harlequin Books requests the pleasure of your company this June in Eternity, Massachusetts, for WEDDINGS, INC.

For generations, couples have been coming to Eternity, Massachusetts, to exchange wedding vows. Legend has it that those married in Eternity's chapel are destined for a lifetime of happiness. And the residents are more than willing to give the legend a hand.

Beginning in June, you can experience the legend of Eternity. Watch for one title per month, across all of the Harlequin series.

HARLEQUIN BOOKS... NOT THE SAME OLD STORY!